Young Believer™
ON TOUR

Liane

Stephen Arterburn
with **Angela Hunt**

TYNDALE KIDS

Tyndale House Publishers, Inc.
Wheaton, Illinois

Visit Tyndale's exciting Web site at www.tyndale.com

Visit the Young Believer Web site at www.youngbeliever.com

Library of Congress Cataloging-in-Publication Data

Arterburn, Stephen, date.
  Liane / Stephen Arterburn and Angela Elwell Hunt.
    p. cm. — (Young believer on tour ; 2)
  Summary: Caught in an unguarded moment, Liane reveals her intellect to a reporter.
  ISBN 0-8423-8336-0 (sc)
[1. Musical groups—Fiction. 2. Christian life—Fiction.] I. Angela Elwell Hunt, date.
II. Title.
PZ7.H9115Li 2004
[Fic]—dc22   2003024230

Printed in the United States of America

10 09 08 07 06 05 04
7   6   5   4   3   2   1

Hold on, he feels your broken heart's pain,

Stand strong, faith holds the key to rescue,

Reach out to love that cleanses your heart stains,

And never stop believin' . . . that God dreams of you.

—Paige Clawson and Shane Clawson

FROM "NEVER STOP BELIEVIN'"
YB2 MUSIC, INC.

August 31

YB2 ENJOYS THE SHOW AS MUCH AS THE CROWD

By Michael Dankin, Weekend Editor
Detroit Register Press

They may be young, but the fresh-faced members of the nation's hottest singing group know how to turn a phrase—and more than a few heads.

When the lights went down last night at Detroit's Palace of Auburn Hills, five young singers appeared under five spotlights on the otherwise dark stage. From the moment the music kicked in and the teens began to move, it was clear YB2 (Young Believers, Second Edition) was planning to have fun—and share it with the crowd.

The group, now traveling fulltime, has polished their presentation to a high gloss. Unlike some bands that play a different set every night, YB2 presents the same concert in each venue—what you get in Detroit is the same thing you get in Pittsburgh, should you be lucky enough to snag a ticket.

The crowd changes every night, though each contains a few common denominators—screaming preteen girls carrying signs proclaiming their love for Shane, Noah, or Josiah, the three resident heartthrobs; toe-tapping grandmoms; and the occasional babe in arms—YB2 wannabes in training.

YB2 opened the night with their newest release, "Never Stop Believin'." To kill time between costume changes, individual group members entertained with brief introductions and stories about their hometowns, ranging from Minneapolis, Minnesota, to Orlando, Florida.

Four members of the band— Shane Clawson, Noah Dudash, Josiah Johnson, and Liane Nelson—exhibited a few funky hiphop moves. Paige Clawson, the group's fifth member and cocomposer of many of their songs, stayed behind the keyboard even during interludes. Smiling at the crowd from behind her trademark sunglasses, her confident image made it difficult to believe that the girl has been blind since birth.

For all their jumping and running and shaking hands with the crowd, these kids can sing. When they gather in their trademark semicircle around the piano for five-part harmony, we are all reminded that they are singers first . . . and the songs have first priority. Their lyrics are about young love, technology, and music, but they also sing about the meaning of life. Heavy stuff for kids.

If you missed them, better call Ticketmaster and reserve your seat for next year. YB2 is taking teen pop to the next level.

Wednesday, September 1

"I'm a girl for all times, livin' in fu-tur-i-si-ty!" Liane Nelson strutted across the stage to the music's pounding beat, then turned on the final downbeat and flung her hand toward the sky. She froze, her head tipped back and her eyes focused on a point in the coliseum's dark ceiling, while she listened to the sounds of air moving through her lungs. Screaming applause rose around her, great whipped waves of it, and she steeled herself against the slightest urge to move until she heard Shane's signal.

Finally, in the first instant the applause began to falter, she heard Shane Clawson's voice. "Cut!"

Immediately Liane and the others snapped erect and moved to the back line. In one practiced motion, they unfastened the Velcro flaps that held the robotic-looking pieces over their black outfits, then yanked them off and tossed the lightweight fiberglass pieces into the darkness beyond the line. Last month RC, their director, had added the pieces as a sign of welcome for Josiah Johnson, the team's newest member, who also happened to have scoliosis. After trying to dance in a brace, even a modified one, Liane understood Josiah's struggle to move in his brace.

At the soundboard, Taz punched the play button. At the first note of the music, the five singers moved into their semicircle position for the final song, "Y B Alone?" This song, the title cut from their first album, had become their unofficial theme. No concert would be complete without it.

As the piano floated a melody across the stage, Liane turned her head, shifting her attention to the brown-haired girl who sat at the keyboard, a top-of-the-line Korg Triton. The epitome of coolness, Paige Clawson flashed a smile beneath her dark glasses as she played. Then she lifted her head and nodded as if she'd just spotted someone special in the audience.

No one would ever guess she was blind just from watching her in concert.

Liane was amazed by her friend. Not only did Paige handle normal life without sight, she also helped write most of the songs they performed.

"You say you're brokenhearted," Paige sang,
"You say you're all alone,
Why let yourself stay in the dark
When there's love enough within his heart
To reach you . . . and hold you."

The music swelled. Liane joined the others in singing soft "ahhs" as she shifted her attention to Shane, commonly known as the biggest heartthrob of the group. He finished the first verse:

"You say your life's a waste of time,
You say you're barely getting by,
Why let yourself listen to the lies
When there's love enough within his eyes
To catch you . . . and keep you."

The drums kicked in, and the funky rhythms began. Liane felt her heart begin to pound with the beat as she lifted her chin.

"'Cause I know," she sang, belting out the words while the others echoed.

"The source of all love
I know
Who puts the power within,
It's not
The star on the TV show,
It's God,
Who created us all."

Grinning, Liane pivoted toward Noah Dudash, the mop-headed California clown who'd been with the group since the beginning, like she had.

"You say you're looking up now," Noah sang, moving to the front line.

"You say you're standing tall,
Be sure you stand on solid ground,
In the Rock alone true hope is found,
And that hope . . . is forever."

The drums kicked, and the entire group finished the chorus with Liane moving out to take the lead.

"'Cause I know—" she lifted her hand and pointed to heaven.

"The source of all love,
I know
Who puts the power within,
It's not
Rich man counting out his dough,
It's God,
Who created us all."

Her heart pounding from the power of the song, Liane swiveled to look at Josiah. He'd been with the group only a month, but Liane already thought of him as a brother.

His pure tenor wafted over the stage: "The One who yearns to love you—"

Liane joined the others in echoing, "Why be alone?"

Josiah grinned at her. "Is always right beside you."

She grinned back. "No, you're not alone."

"So never stop believing—"

"He'll never let you go."

"He's calling out your name—"

"Now and forever . . ."

One more time—as one, Shane, Liane, Noah, and

Josiah moved from the back line to the front, stepping as close to the screaming fans as they dared. Noah led off on the final chorus while the others echoed.

"'Cause I know," he sang, pointing to his brain.
"The source of all love
I know
Who puts the power within,
It's not
Experts who are in the know,
It's God,
Who created us all."

The song ended; they froze in their choreographed positions while the applause erupted from the enthusiastic crowd. Liane closed her eyes as happiness filled her. Some days she might be tired, she might be sick, she might be depressed, but when she stood on the stage and heard this kind of applause, all her negative feelings melted away.

She *loved* her life with YB2.

"Cut!" Shane's voice cut through the roar. "And bow. One!"

Stepping back, Liane caught Paige's and Noah's hands. They had perfected an eight-count bow—after Shane's initial "one," they took two counts to grab each other's hands (the extra beat was necessary to guide Paige from her place behind the keyboard to the back line). On "four" they lifted their linked hands; on "five" they bent at the waist and swept their heads to their knees. They counted "six" in the bent position, on "seven" they straightened and lifted their arms again, and on "eight" they returned to their starting position. They bowed as many times as it took to satisfy the audience—tonight looked like a five-bow night—then, if the applause wasn't dying, they kicked into another chorus of "Y B Alone?" as an encore.

After the encore and half a dozen more bows, the five singers linked hands and ran off the stage.

As they moved out of the bright lights and into the cloaking darkness, Liane took deep gulps of air. Noah dropped her hand and hurried off with the guys, but she kept a firm grip on Paige and led her toward the black curtains that separated the public areas from the back-stage crew.

Paige managed fine in almost every situation, and she didn't like to ask for help. Liane admired her friend's independence, but even sighted people could use a help-ing hand in the chaos of a packed coliseum.

Safely behind the black fabric wall that divided them from the demanding fans, Liane linked her arm through Paige's and slowed her step. A pair of security guards nodded as she passed, and she managed to give them a tired smile in return.

"Come on, Paige." She turned toward the hallway where their dressing room was located. "Ready to change?"

How many dressing rooms had she visited over the last few months? Liane had joined YB2 in the group's first official year. Happily, RC had asked her to come back for a second year, along with Shane, Paige, and Noah. Josiah had joined them last month at rehearsal camp in Orlando, replacing Vance Gerkin, who had made some pretty serious mistakes and had to leave the band.

Liane thought of Vance nearly every day. The group's incredible success apparently had gone to Vance's head. During the summer break he'd gone to a party and gotten drunk—which was bad enough—but then he'd tried to slug some reporter who was trying to get a picture of the famous Vance Gerkin making a fool of himself.

So he wasn't the famous Vance Gerkin anymore. Liane felt sorry for him in a way—he'd paid a big price for messing up—but RC had warned them all. "You are living in a goldfish bowl," he'd told them time and time again. "People are watching your every move. And since we stand for something positive, people are going to be watching us even more closely than they watch other groups."

Liane was used to people watching her—some of the guys complained about not being able to go out in public without being recognized, but sometimes she liked the attention. And she wasn't recognized very often when she was alone—if she went out in a baseball cap and sunglasses, most people figured she was just one of the girls from the neighborhood.

But when they went out as a group . . . that's when things got sticky. Every American girl between the ages of eight and sixteen seemed to be in love with Shane,

Josiah, or Noah, and *everybody* loved YB2. So if they were all together, or if they went somewhere in their performance clothes, it was impossible to do something as simple as visit the restroom without causing a scene.

Life in the goldfish bowl could be frustrating at times . . . especially when she just wanted to be alone to read or think. People always wanted to see them, hear them, touch them. Once, after the bus made a quick stop at a McDonald's in Michigan, Shane's empty Quarter Pounder carton turned up on eBay. Newspaper and magazine reporters wanted to know what they thought about all kinds of issues, and Liane was amazed that any goofball comment from a kid in YB2 could make headlines in *Tiger Beat* or *Teen People*.

With her arm linked through Paige's, Liane moved through the civic center's wide halls, then found the door labeled "YB2 Female Dressing Room." The security guard stepped aside as she and Paige approached, then he reached out to help her open the door.

After thanking him, Liane walked Paige to a sofa against the wall, then sank into a chair before a mirrored vanity. She stared at her reflection, where sweat had smeared her mascara and created smudges under her eyes. "Man, it was hot tonight. I thought I was going to melt into a puddle out there!"

"It *was* hot," Paige agreed, pulling off her glasses. "And all this makeup can't be good for my skin. Lee, do you see any zits on my nose?"

Liane grinned as she leaned toward her friend. "Honestly, I can't see a thing under that pancake makeup."

Paige sighed as she stood and reached for the white-tipped cane she'd left on the sofa. "I'm going to wash up and change. Will you be ready to go to the bus in a while?"

"Yeah, I'll go with you." Liane peered back into the mirror, half-expecting to see bags under her fourteen-year-old eyes. YB2 had been on the road for nearly two weeks, and she was beginning to feel the need for a break. "I just want to curl up on the bus and go to sleep."

"Sorry." Paige's voice floated from the back of the room where she'd left her clothes in a locker. "We have an interview, remember? Some guy from *People* magazine."

Liane groaned. She'd forgotten about the special arrangement *People* had made with RC. YB2 had been interviewed lots of times in *Teen People,* but now the adult magazine was interested in them. Instead of sending one writer to a press conference with twenty other reporters, *People* had asked if one of their journalists could travel with YB2 for twenty-four hours. RC had liked the reporter's unique approach, so the deal was made. The guy had attended the concert tonight and would soon be boarding the bus with the singers.

He was lucky he'd picked this night. Sometimes after a concert they had to sit for interviews or give autographs for long lines of fans who had won local radio or television contests. But tonight they were on a tight schedule, so they had to move out as soon as possible.

Liane had thought she'd find travel boring, but she'd been pleasantly surprised by life on the bus. Though the group sometimes flew to special concerts and TV events, they usually traveled in two semitrailers and a shiny black bus with a simple shooting star on the side. The trailers carried the lights, stage equipment, and audio equipment; the bus transported the singers and their luggage. RC was always saying he wanted them to feel like they had a place to crash, so the roomy vehicle had become their home away from home.

Liane pulled a washcloth from her makeup case. "I forgot all about the guy from *People* . . . and I'm still not sure I understand why he wants to ride with us. I mean, it's not like he'll enjoy hearing the guys burp and carry on like they do."

Paige laughed. "He said he wanted to see the real YB2. But the real us might be more than he bargained for."

"I'll say."

Liane stood and slipped out of her performance clothes, then pulled her sweatpants and a faded shirt from the bottom of her tote bag. This outfit would never fly if they were going to appear in public, but only the group members and the guy from *People* would see her tonight. She and Paige would exit through a back door and leave the arena in the bus.

After changing, Liane washed the makeup from her face and brushed her teeth. If all went well, she'd be asleep within a couple of hours.

She paused in the middle of smearing moisturizer on her face. "You need any help, Paige?"

"I'm okay." The girl turned from the sink where she stood, displaying freshly scrubbed skin. She had changed out of her performance outfit, too, and now wore baggy jeans and a fleece T-shirt.

Liane packed her overnight bag with her toiletries, hung all the pieces of both girls' performance outfits in a garment bag, then checked the room for any other personal items. When she was sure nothing would be left behind, she hoisted her small suitcase to her shoulder, then hooked the hanging bag over her right hand.

"Ready to hit the bus?"

Paige picked up her cane and her overnight bag. "Ready as I'll ever be. And I think—" she yawned— "I'm ready for bed, too."

"Yeah—let's hope this reporter guy doesn't try to gab with us tonight."

Holding on to one another, the two girls left the room.

2

Liane had never thought she'd look forward to
hours of peace and quiet, but after a long concert and
an even longer day, all she wanted to do was sleep.

After helping Paige into the bus, Liane climbed in
after her and stopped to say hi to their driver, Larry
Forsyth. Larry had slept during their concert, but now
he looked wide awake, having been wired by coffee and
refreshed by a shower. His thin hair had been combed
into a perfect wave atop his head, and the scent of Old
Spice rose from his pink skin.

Liane patted him on the shoulder. "Ready to roll,
Larry?"

"Ready, Freddy. As soon as RC gives the order."

Liane paused to check out the bus. The boys were on
board already—Shane had plopped down in a pair of seats
in front, propping his back against the window wall while

his long legs hung over the armrest and into the aisle. Buried in a book, he didn't even look up as she edged past his size twelve sneakers. Josiah had curled up with his pillow in the seat opposite Shane, and his eyes were already at half-mast. Noah stood in the middle of the seat section, his arms braced against the luggage compartment railing. He didn't look at all sleepy, so Liane made a mental note: *Don't sit near Noah unless you want to be awake all night.*

Larry looked back when Liane paused in the aisle. "Whaddya say, Missy? Gonna sit up here and talk to me for a while?"

"Not tonight, Larry. I'm pooped."

"Go on, then, and reserve yourself a bunk. Should be a quiet ride on the interstate tonight."

Liane searched her memory as she made her way through the bus. Their next concert was . . . where? They'd been on the road so long she never knew where they were unless she looked at the schedule. One city pretty much looked like another, and nearly all the arenas had the same floor plan. She'd sat in so many dressing rooms with painted concrete block walls that they were beginning to run together in her brain.

Thank goodness for the bus, their cozy home away from home. YB2's touring vehicle had been purchased used before the group hit it big, but RC loved it and wouldn't trade it, even though now they could afford something more plush. He also preferred bus travel over flying. "Why should we fly?" he'd asked the reporter who wondered why they traveled in a renovated Greyhound. "This works just fine for us, and it gives the kids a private home on wheels. Besides, it's educational—we're getting a great look at America as we travel through it."

Liane liked flying, but she also liked the bus. The vehicle was divided into thirds, with almost all the comforts of home. Twenty regular bus seats filled the section behind the driver, in ten sets of two, and a small drop-down screen in the ceiling connected to a DVD player in case they wanted to watch movies. RC had stocked the bus with video games, too, and each member of YB2 had been given an iPod, a slim silver music player that could fit into their pocket and hold 10,000 songs downloaded from an Internet subscription service.

In the bus's center section, two tables with rounded ends and bench seating provided a place where the group could gather for meals, meetings, studying, or games. Paige often set her keyboard there and worked on music as the big bus ate up the miles. A small microwave in the overhead rack allowed them to warm up snacks whenever the munchies struck.

The back section, next to the only restroom, was affectionately known as the "sleeping car." Four padded bunks had been built into each wall, and Liane had to admit they reminded her of the narrow bunks she'd once seen in a submarine movie. The kids could slide into them easily enough, but they couldn't sit upright without bumping their heads on the bunk above.

Their luggage traveled in storage bays beneath the bus while their more personal belongings rode in the overhead bins above the seats.

After scooting past Noah, Liane bent to peek into the lowest bunk on the right side of the bus. Paige lay there, her head on her pillow and her blanket pulled up around her shoulders. The girl could crash almost instantly and sleep through anything.

Although Liane felt exhausted, she was still too wired to head off to bed. She walked back to the tables, then sank onto a bench and rested her head on her folded arms. She didn't want to go to sleep unless she knew she wouldn't be awakened, and the odds of that were slim, at least until they were well on their way. RC often called them together for an after-concert huddle, and he might still tonight.

She had drifted into a light doze when the director's voice called her awake. "Hey, gang. Can I have your attention for a moment?"

Liane lifted her head and squinted toward the door. RC stood at the top of the bus steps, and a dark-haired man in a leather jacket stood behind him in the doorway. The stranger wore jeans and a YB2 T-shirt.

She groaned softly. The guy had already snagged the interview—so why was he trying to impress them by wearing one of their T-shirts?

RC caught her eye. "Is Paige in the back?"

She nodded. "She's asleep."

"Will you wake her, please?"

Liane went to the back and knelt by Paige's side. She shook the girl awake. "Paige—your dad wants us."

Paige grunted a moment, then sighed and lifted her head. She held out her hand and grumbled as Liane pulled her out of the narrow space. "I forgot—it's the reporter, right?"

"Looks like it."

By the time they returned to the table area, the stranger had taken a seat at the far end. Shane, Josiah, Taz, and Noah sat at the table with the reporter, so Paige and Liane slipped into two empty places on the opposite side.

"This is Huck Phillips, from *People* magazine." RC stood and gestured toward the man, who nodded and smiled. "He wanted to experience life with you guys for twenty-four hours, so we figured this was a good place to start. I've promised that he can ask you a few questions now, then I'm going to let you all get some rest—in fact, I'm going to insist upon it. Tomorrow, though, I'd appreciate it if you'd give Mr. Phillips as much time as he needs to get an accurate story."

Liane forced a smile as she looked at the reporter. This was the part of being famous that most people didn't know about. Sometimes, even when they were so tired their teeth hurt, they had to smile and make conversation and laugh and pretend to be all the wonderful things everyone thought they were. If one of them was suffering from a headache or the stomach flu, the rule still stuck: smile and wave and sign autographs and be nice. Because people would cling to their five-minute impression instead of believing all the previous press they had heard.

"Hi, everyone." Huck Phillips smiled around the circle. "First, I want to thank you for giving me this opportunity. I'm sure it's a pain for someone to barge in on your private time, but we want to give our readers a peek into the real people behind the YB2 faces. So I promise not to be a bother or get in the way—I just want to hang out and be a fly on the wall, okay?"

Liane lifted a brow. Most reporters came in with a list of basically the same questions for each team member. When they spoke to her, they wanted to know how old she was, how she got to be in YB2, what she wanted to do when she left the group, and how she liked being a four-teen-year-old superstar. She'd answered those questions so many times she thought she should print her answers on a sheet of paper and save people the trouble of asking.

RC tilted his head toward the reporter. "Do you want to ask anything while they're all here?"

Mr. Phillips shook his head. "I've read the press kit bios on all of them, so I think I've got the basics covered. Honestly, I just want to hang out. That's it."

RC's gaze scanned the group. "All right, then. You know what that means—just be yourselves."

Liane gave him a small, tired smile. They *did* know what that meant, so they'd be themselves, only nicer. One of the infamous "Ron's Rules" dealt with outsiders— whenever anybody outside the group was present, everybody had to be on their best behavior. That meant no roughhousing, no name-calling, and no food fights.

Liane twirled a finger around a strand of her hair. "So . . . is there anything else?"

RC drew a deep breath. "Only a little critique of the concert. Paige, honey, you have to remember to keep your chin up when you're singing solos. When you point your chin down, your face gets lost in the shadows. It's hard for the camera to pick you up."

The corners of Paige's mouth drooped. "I don't want to look like Stevie Wonder."

Noah snickered. "How would you know what Stevie Wonder looks like?"

Paige quirked a brow in Noah's direction. "I've heard what he looks like. And I'm afraid if I lift my chin too high, people will make fun of me."

RC reached out to pat Paige's hand. "You don't look like Stevie Wonder, hon. Just remember to keep your chin elevated a *little,* not a lot."

He looked around the table as if trying to remember items on a mental list, and Liane caught her breath when his gaze crossed hers. RC's corrections were almost always gentle, but it still stung to receive one. They all thought he was great, and the idea of doing something to disappoint him . . . well, she'd rather lose her voice for a month.

She flinched when RC looked at her and snapped his fingers. "I nearly forgot. Lee—we need you to memorize some Spanish lyrics."

She blinked. "What?"

"For the Latin Grammy Awards on the fourteenth. We'll be singing 'Y B Alone?' but I want you to sing the verses in Spanish. The others will back you up."

She looked at Shane, who grinned as if to say *Aren't you the lucky one?,* then she looked at Noah. "Why am I singing their parts?"

"Because no one else speaks Spanish."

She laughed. "I don't speak Spanish, either."

"But you have an especially good ear, you're a great mimic, and I just know you'll pick it up in no time. I have no doubt you'll be fine."

She looked at Paige, who wore a grin the size of Texas. Sometimes she wished her friend could see just so they could trade understanding looks whenever RC came up with one of his crazy ideas.

"Okay." Ron placed his hands on the tabletop. "That's all the business for tonight. Lee, I'll give you those lyrics as soon as Rhonda faxes them to me. Oh— I nearly forgot something else. We had mail waiting at the civic center office." He turned to rummage through the overhead bin, then pulled a large manila envelope from his briefcase. After unhooking the envelope's clasp, he slid out a stack of envelopes and flipped through them. "Lee, here's a letter for you. Shane, one for you, too. From Orlando."

Liane grinned as Shane's cheeks darkened. Earlier this week she'd been teasing him about the girl who lived next door to the YB2 complex in Orlando. Shane kept insisting they were just friends, but she seemed to write him a lot.

"Noah, a letter for you. Joe, five letters for you."

Their newest team member grinned as he gathered up his mail. "My sisters," he explained, holding up one envelope that had been addressed in crayon. "Mom makes them write me at least once a week."

Liane looked at the letter in her hand. The envelope bore her mother's handwriting and the word *Freckles,* the special code word that would ensure that the letter escaped the mountain of fan mail. Melisma Records had established a special post office box for YB2 fan correspondence, but some fans still managed to discover the group's Orlando mailing address. For security reasons, each team member had to choose a special code word, and only mail with that code on the envelope was forwarded to the group on the road.

Liane had chosen the name of her cat as her code word. She ripped the envelope open, then smiled when a half dozen photographs of Freckles spilled onto her lap. "E-mail would be easier," she mumbled.

"But snail mail is better." Josiah held up a colorful drawing from one of his little sisters. The girl had drawn six stick figures, obviously the entire family, and one of them wore a scoliosis brace—that would be Josiah.

"Yeah." Liane nodded as she rubbed her finger over the glossy photo of her cat. An unexpected knot of homesickness clogged her throat. "I guess you're right."

3

After Ron dismissed the meeting, Larry pulled the big bus onto the road and turned off the overhead lights. Paige returned to her bunk, and RC sat up front to read his mail. The reporter, Mr. Phillips, sat at the table looking through a YB2 press kit like a student cramming for an exam.

Settling into a seat by the window, Noah clicked on the overhead light, then slid his thumbnail under the edge of his letter from home. His mom was as regular as a sunrise, writing him all the news from San Diego at least once a week.

He was glad she didn't send her wordy notes through e-mail. He liked letters. On long bus rides when he was tired of listening to music and playing video games, he liked to reread letters from home.

His father never wrote. Five years before, when Noah

Liane

was nine, the man had packed up and moved to Las Vegas without so much as a backward glance. Noah's mom had been heartbroken, and Noah had had a hard time believing his dad actually meant to stay away.

He believed it now. Noah hadn't heard a word from his dad in five years. Oh, each December a Christmas package arrived from Las Vegas, something wrapped in shiny red or green paper, but Noah never even opened the gifts. He threw the first one in the trash, then felt guilty about wasting it. Every year since, he'd given the packages to a neighborhood toy drive.

His mom had never gotten anything but a divorce. He looked again at her letter and thumped it against his palm. This one felt heavier than usual, and he looked again at the envelope before pulling out the pages. Beneath his address she had written "Justus," his code word and the name of his mastiff, a dog that weighed more than Noah and his mother combined. She usually threw a few pictures of the big boy into each envelope, but there were no photos this time—just three pages, covered front and back with her loopy handwriting.

Surrounded by the nighttime silence of the bus, he hunched low in the seat and began to read.

Dearest Noah,

I hardly know where to begin. If this isn't a good time for you to read some hard news, Son, put this letter down and come back to it when you have free time. I don't want to upset you before a performance.

Liane

Gulping back a sudden rise of fear, Noah lifted his head and looked around the bus. RC had stood up and disappeared into the back; so had Paige and Josiah. Liane was sitting by the window, her eyes wide and focused on the night outside; Shane was sitting in front of her with his nose buried in a book. The overhead light shone on Shane's dark hair, creating a glow like a fake halo.

Noah looked out at the road. With Larry at the helm they were flying through the night, skimming past the broken highway lines as if they were on a magic carpet. The crackle of static came from the front, then Larry tuned in a country station and began to sing.

Nobody ever looked forward to bad news, but Noah figured this was as good a time as any to hear it. Lowering his head, he kept reading.

Honey, you know Justus's hips have never been good. Well, his front elbow joints were getting bad, too, and lately he'd been having trouble going up and down the porch steps. Even though he was a relatively young dog, I knew the end was getting close. Last week, it came.

Noah lowered the pages as his throat closed up. He turned toward the window and stared at the watery eyes in the center of his reflection.

His mother said "it came."

No.

Liane

It wasn't time for Justus to go. He was only five, and he was supposed to live at least ten years. Noah had felt terrible about going away to sing in YB2 and leaving Justus at home, but he'd promised the dog he'd be back in plenty of time to be around . . . later.

For Jussy, later would never come.

He looked back down at the letter, but couldn't read the words through his tears. Lowering his head still further, he dashed the tears away and tried to focus on his mother's writing.

Last week Jussy went outside and climbed into the pool—you know how he always loved the water. I thought maybe the water would feel good on his aching hips, but when he tried to get out, he couldn't manage the steps. I got in the pool and put a towel around him, then tried to pull him out—but the towel rubbed against his elbows.

He cried, Noah—and you know how strong he was; he never cried. So I called the vet and told them I needed help.

They came, sweetheart. The vet rushed right over with two helpers, and together we all got Jussy out of the pool. He was so tired by that time; he just lay down on the pavement and panted. I knelt by his big head and rubbed his ears, promising him that things would be okay. While the vet prepped him for the shot that would put him to sleep, I leaned forward and whispered that we'd see him in heaven. I don't know for sure about such things, but in that moment it felt right to say it.

And soon it was all over. He didn't suffer, Noah— he just slowed his breathing and began to snore, then he stopped making any noise at all. Then the vet said he was gone. I didn't know what to do next, but the vet gave me the number for a pet funeral home. They came out and picked Jussy up, and I'm supposed to drive out there next week and pick up the urn with his ashes. I'm not sure what we should do with it—but I'll let you decide. He was your dog, your buddy. I'm so sorry he left without being able to tell you good-bye.

Noah crumpled the letter in his hands, his eyes stinging. This wasn't fair! His dog wasn't supposed to die, not like this! And his mom—how could she have killed his dog without asking him first?

Burying his face in his hands, Noah bit back sobs as tears watered his hands.

4

"Mind if I sit here?"

Liane looked up as Huck Phillips gestured to the empty seat next to her. Part of her wished she'd thought to block the seat with her purse or tote bag, but now that he'd asked it'd be rude to refuse.

She sighed. She should have gone back to the bunks right after RC broke up the meeting, but the dark sky had called to her, and she loved looking out the wide windows at night.

She shrugged. "Fine by me."

The man sank into the seat, then fidgeted a moment until he had reclined the back to a comfortable position. "This is quite a bus—do you enjoy traveling in it?"

She shrugged again. "It's okay. It can be a hassle when we get to a town and somebody needs to run to the drugstore or something, but most of the time it's great."

Nodding, Mr. Phillips folded his hands across his chest. "So . . . what do you like most about traveling with the country's hottest group?"

She turned toward the window so he couldn't see her smile. Maybe he thought she wouldn't realize he had sat here with every intention of beginning his interviews tonight, but she knew the difference between conversation and nosing around for a story.

"I like the people." She met his direct gaze. "And I like being able to relax when the concert's over. We work hard, Mr. Phillips, and sometimes we need a little time to unwind. It's an exhausting concert, and sometimes we need our space, you know?"

A slow smile spread across his face. "So . . . you'd rather I didn't interview you now."

She nodded. "Nothing personal, you know. It's just . . . late."

"Believe me, I understand."

They rode without speaking for a few minutes, the silence broken only by the noise coming from Larry's country radio station.

"I know what it's like," Phillips said, his eyes half-closed, "to wear a mask all the time. It can be really tiring. You get to the point where you can't wait to take it off and just be yourself."

Liane turned back to the window but didn't reply. The man hadn't actually asked an interview question, but she still felt like he was trying to put words in her mouth. If she agreed with him, he could write,

"Liane Nelson admits that wearing a mask can be difficult. . . ."

She lifted her gaze to the stars. Maybe if she could change the subject, this man would forget about his article . . . or go away and question someone else.

"Do you like astronomy?" She bent her head low to catch the widest view of the night sky. "You can't see many stars from the bus except when all the lights are off."

Mr. Phillips made a rumbling sound deep in his throat. Maybe she could put him to sleep.

"I like looking at the stars," she said. "It makes me wonder about the creation of the universe—are you familiar with the prevailing theories?"

Mr. Phillips coughed. "Yeah. Yes, I think so."

"Most scientists credit Edwin Hubble for the leading theory," she continued, smiling to herself. Last night Noah had been unable to fall asleep, but she'd started talking about the origin of outer space and he'd been snoring within ten minutes. "Hubble proved that the universe is expanding from a common origin, and I like that idea. I believe in an intelligent Creator, and it only makes sense that God could use whatever method he chose to create the universe."

She risked a glance at the reporter. As she had hoped, his eyes were beginning to glaze.

"Before you can begin to understand the structure of the universe," she continued, looking back toward the stars, "you have to understand black holes—you know, the sort of vacuum that results from a large star burning all its fuel and exploding into a supernova. The remaining material shrinks down to a neutron star, and if it's big enough, it becomes a black hole. Black holes produce a gravitational force so strong not even light can escape them. Sort of like a big vacuum cleaner in space, swallowing light and sound and anything else that comes along."

She paused, but the man didn't answer. She hoped he had fallen asleep, but when she looked over she found him watching her with wide eyes. "You actually understand all that stuff?"

"What's not to understand?" Shrugging, she turned back to the window. "Astronomy is no harder to comprehend than the subatomic world. In fact, there are so many parallels. In atomic structure, for instance, the nucleus is a tightly packed ball of protons and neutrons with electrons spinning all around it. In an analogous sort of way, it's just like a black hole, but in miniature." She laughed softly. "Of course, when you get into the study of quarks, things can get a little confusing. A neutron is composed of one 'up' quark and two 'down' quarks, while a proton is composed of two 'up' quarks and one 'down' quark. You probably know that the transfer mediums within protons and neutrons are particles called gluons . . ."

A soft sound fluttered near her left ear. She turned and found her pupil snoring softly, his mouth only inches from her shoulder.

"The universe," she whispered, slowly standing, "stretches in infinite directions and is filled with ancient black holes." Carefully, she stepped over her sleeping seatmate's legs. "Some scientists have claimed that the universe will continue into infinity, but I'm content to let God decide what he wants to do with it."

She exhaled in relief when she reached the aisle without waking Huck Phillips. A tiny flicker of guilt fluttered through her—she *could* have been more cooperative— but surely RC didn't expect them to take interviews at nearly midnight.

She laughed softly. She'd given him a pile of useless information, so unless he was writing an article on the solar system, he probably wouldn't have much to say about her.

And that was cool. . . . It would serve him right for trying to launch a sneak-attack interview.

5

Liane had just stretched out on a bunk when she heard something that sounded like hiccups coming from somewhere in the dimness. She looked at Paige, who slept on the bunk beneath her, then looked at the bunks on the opposite wall. Josiah had stretched out and was already dead to the world, Taz and RC were talking about sound equipment at the tables, and she'd left Noah and Shane up front . . . unless one of them had slipped by her while she was stargazing.

She thrust her head into the heavy silence and listened more closely. She heard a sniffle, then the sound of tissues being pulled from a box. So the sound was coming from the bathroom. And if that was a teary sniffle she'd heard, then those weren't hiccups at all.

She swung her legs off the bunk and leaned forward into the darkness. What should she do?

A moment later the bathroom door opened. The light inside flared for a moment, revealing Noah's angular frame. He closed the door, leaving them in semidarkness, and Liane stood to touch his shoulder. "You okay, Noah?"

He jumped. "Good grief, Lee, you nearly scared me to death."

"Sorry." She studied his face. "You want to talk about it?"

He looked away for a moment, and in the dim light from the front she saw the glimmer of tears on his cheek. "I'm okay."

"You sure don't seem okay."

He didn't look at her, but kept his eyes focused on the aisle leading to the front of the bus. He might have stood there all night, but she waved toward the seats. "Come on, Noah. Let's go up front where we can talk."

She led the way, pulling him behind her like a small child. She slid into one of seats by the window, and he sat down next to her.

For a long while they said nothing, then Noah pitched forward, burying his face in his folded arms. She watched, horrified, as his shoulders began to shake with silent sobs.

What could make a guy like Noah cry? Liane searched her memory—RC hadn't been upset with Noah; he hadn't pulled him aside for any kind of lecture. Noah didn't have a girlfriend, so this couldn't be girl trouble, and he didn't have any brothers or sisters. . . .

She folded her arms and dropped her head next to his. "What is it, dude? You can tell me."

He didn't look up for a full minute, then he finally lifted his head long enough to pull an envelope from his jeans pocket. He dropped it on the seat next to her and buried his head again. "Read it," he said, his voice muffled from beneath his arms.

Feeling partly curious and partly concerned, Liane opened the letter and began to read. The reason for Noah's tears became immediately clear—everybody in the group knew how much he loved his dog. The big, lovable goof was a celebrity in his own right—he'd worked as the mascot for Noah's middle school, he'd appeared on local television news programs back in San Diego, and the year before Noah joined YB2, he and his dog had been invited to New York to appear on *LIVE with Regis and Kelly*. After a hilarious weigh-in on the TV show, Noah's dog had been unofficially declared the second-biggest dog in America . . . but now he was gone.

"Noah, I'm so sorry." Liane slipped her arm around her friend's shoulder. "I know how much you loved that dog."

"He was my best friend." Noah lifted his head long enough to swipe at the tears on his cheeks. "The funny thing is, I ought to have hated him. My dad got him for me right before he left us—I think he meant Justus to be some kind of stand-in for him. But I couldn't help but love the big doofus, and now that he's gone . . . I don't have anything from my dad."

Liane squeezed his arm, as her heart overflowed with sympathy. Her parents were happily married; she couldn't imagine what Noah had gone through when his dad left. Obviously, he hid a lot of pain beneath his jokester personality.

"I'm so sorry," she whispered, not wanting to wake the others. Her gaze fell upon Huck Phillips's brown hair against the back of a seat ahead of them—*this* was a story Noah didn't need splattered across the pages of *People* magazine.

"I can't imagine what you must be feeling." She lowered her head so her words would reach his ear alone. "And I know you're going to be sad for a while. I'll pray for you."

Noah grimaced. "What good will prayers do now? Justus is gone. My mom killed him. By now she probably has his ashes sitting in a jar on the front porch."

"That's not fair, Noah. Don't you think your mom had a hard time with it, too? I'm sure she did everything she could, and so did the vet. He was so big . . . it's not like he was the kind of dog you could pick up and carry when he needed to go outside."

Noah didn't answer, but Liane could tell her words had struck home. His chin quivered, but he kept his eyes on the overhead light burning above Shane's head.

Liane searched her brain for an idea. She had read several interesting books for her online psychology class, and one of them suggested that grief could and should be channeled into something productive . . .

"Hey, I have an idea. You know how you felt about Justus, right?"

Noah nodded.

"And you hate to let him go, right?"

Another nod.

"Well . . . you don't have to let him go. Why don't you take those feelings and put them into something you can use to remember him? A story, maybe, or a poem. Or maybe you can write a song about him. That way, every time you read the story or the poem, you'll think of all those good memories of him. And as long as you remember him, it'll be like he never really left you."

When he swiveled to face her, Liane thought he was going to tell her that she'd just suggested the craziest idea he had ever heard. His brow lowered, his lower lip jutted forward, but all he said was, "I'm not good with words. There's no way I can write a story."

"A poem, then. It could be really short."

His forehead crinkled. "You don't get it—I have dyslexia. Everything I try to write comes out backward. I've always been terrible with words and stories and books. I couldn't write a poem if my life depended on it."

"Write a song, then. You're a musician, so surely you can write a song."

He sat back, his eyes squinting, then nodded. "Yeah. Why not? Paige and Shane write songs all the time. I've seen them come up with a chorus over lunch."

"You could do it, too. It doesn't have to be anything complicated, just something about Justus."

"Yeah." He swiped at his cheeks again, but the tears were no longer flowing. "I could write a song. I have my guitar on the bus, so I could strum out a few chords—"

"You see?" Liane gave him a wide smile. "You can do it, I know you can. And when the song is done, you can sing it for everyone in the group. And then they'll know what you're feeling."

He looked at her, his eyes gleaming in the light. "That's good 'cause I don't think I could talk about it without crying. And I can't let them see me cry."

Liane nodded. She didn't know who invented that silly rule about guys not being allowed to cry, but Noah and Shane seemed to think it was written in stone. Sometimes she thought they'd rather lose an arm than shed a tear in public.

She gave him a small smile. "So . . . it's a cool idea?"

"Yeah, it's cool. I'll start on it tomorrow. And Liane, will you do me a favor?"

"Name it."

"Will you . . . tell the others about Jussy for me? I don't think I can talk about it. Not for a while, at least."

"Sure I will." Touched by his request, Liane leaned down to look him in the eye. "Now if you'll let me out, I think I'd like to get a little sleep. It's been a long day."

Noah swiveled his long legs out of the way, letting her slip by, then hunkered low in the seat again.

A pleasant sense of accomplishment washed over Liane as she made her way to her bunk. Long ago she had decided that intelligence was useless unless you used it to help people, and tonight she had found a simple way to help a friend.

On nights like this, she was grateful for her brains.

6

Weighed down with sadness, Noah curled up in the double seat, grateful for the stillness on the bus. Beneath the floor, the diesel engines purred like kittens. The sound usually lulled him to sleep within minutes of lying down, but tonight his heart was too heavy.

He couldn't imagine his home without Justus. He didn't think much about the dog when he was on the road, but his mind couldn't imagine going home, opening the door, and seeing . . . no dog. Every time Noah had come home, Justus had been waiting there, a 275-pound mass of happiness. His tail, which could beat dents in the wall, would whip back and forth, and his eyes would light up like little lanterns above a goofy dog-smile.

Noah rubbed his hand over his face, wishing he could wipe all the traces of sadness from his mind. He was going to miss that dog something fierce. At home, the

Liane

touch of Jussy's tongue woke Noah up every morning, and the sound of his snoring sent Noah to sleep every night. The dog was like the honorary mayor of the neighborhood; everyone knew him and loved to pause and pet the big lug. He had stopped traffic on his visit to New York City—on every potty run to Central Park, he'd been surrounded by curious tourists and nosy New York natives.

Since joining YB2 Noah had achieved a certain amount of fame, but he'd had to *sing* to get it. Justus had been famous just for being Justus—and he had loved every minute of his life.

Except maybe at the end.

Noah closed his eyes, suddenly thankful he hadn't been home the day Justus couldn't climb out of the pool. His mom must have been frantic with no one to help her, and even the two of them would have struggled to lift Justus.

His mom had done the right thing. He didn't want to admit it, but Liane was right. Mom had said Justus cried, and the huge animal hadn't even done that the time Noah had accidentally shut the car door on his tail.

Noah squinched his eyes shut as a fresh wave of tears blurred his vision. Thank goodness his mother had written instead of telling him the news on the phone. He would have yelled, reacting in anger, and his mom would have been crushed. Noah loved Justus to death, but his mom loved the dog, too. Since Noah had joined YB2, Justus had become the man of the house, his mom's companion and protector.

He'd have to call her, later, when he could talk about Justus without crying. He'd thank her for writing a tough letter.

Noah rolled onto his side, pillowing his head on his bent arm. Man, this felt terrible. Awful. He'd never had anyone close to him die before. One of his gerbils had died when he was a kid, but a gerbil was nothing like a dog. A dog went everywhere with you, heard all your secrets, and sat and listened to you play your guitar even when you were lousy and fumbling all over the place. You could be in a bad mood and ignore your dog, but still he'd come over and rest his head on your knee and remind you he loved you. When Noah was on the computer e-mailing his friends, Justus would come over and use his head to push Noah's arm away from the keyboard. He'd keep pushing until Noah stopped and hugged his neck, then he'd return to his favorite corner and plop back down, content for the rest of the night.

Noah drew a deep breath and rubbed his eyes. He'd have to stop thinking like this or he'd drive himself crazy. Maybe Liane had the right idea—he should concentrate on creating something positive so some good could come out of this awful pain.

But brainy Liane had no idea how bad he was with words. All the way through elementary school he'd gotten special help for his learning disabilities. Even now Aunt Rhonda worked with him to make sure his studies were designed for his special needs—he took oral tests and listened to most of his textbooks on tape. Words made sense when they entered his ears, but his eyes seemed to jumble things up.

So . . . maybe he could write a song. Songs were nothing but music with words, and songs had more to do with the ear than the eyes. Poetry wasn't his thing, but tomorrow he could take out his guitar and write a song for Justus.

He closed his eyes as a sense of warmth rose from his belly and began to travel through his veins. Things would be okay. It felt good to have a goal. And he was grateful to Liane for giving it to him. She was abso-tively *brilliant*.

Tomorrow he'd get busy writing his song. Tonight, though, he wanted to lie here and miss Jussy.

7

"Hey, Lee."

She pulled the headphones away from her ears as Josiah tugged on her sleeve.

"Yeah?"

"We're at a grocery store. You want any snacks?"

Liane turned toward the wide windows and cast a longing glance at the store. In her first year with YB2 she'd have been one of the first off the bus. She loved combing the cosmetics aisles and skimming through the magazines . . . but these days they couldn't stay in a grocery store long without being recognized, especially if they got off the bus in a group. Josiah could manage to go out because he was new, and Larry was always good about bringing back anything she wanted. Still . . .

She gave Josiah a rueful smile. "Can't think of anything I need. But thanks for asking."

"Okay." He slipped his hands into his pockets as a deep blush rose from his cheeks. The kid turned red every time he talked to her—what was that about?

She watched as Josiah, Larry, and RC got off the bus and headed across the parking lot. She couldn't tell where the bus had stopped—someplace between Indiana and St. Louis, she guessed. They'd performed last night at the Market Square Arena in Indianapolis, and according to the schedule, they'd be in St. Louis in a few hours. They'd have the night off, thank goodness, but tomorrow they were supposed to perform before a sold-out crowd at the St. Louis Arena.

She looked around the bus. Paige sat in a front seat with her portable keyboard in her lap. She looked a little odd playing a silent keyboard, but as long as she wore her headphones, she could make music without disturbing anyone else. Shane slept in the seat behind her, his long legs spilling into the aisle and his head propped against the window. His chin jutted into the air at an odd angle, and even from where she sat Liane could tell he was sleeping with his mouth open.

She suppressed a giggle. *Tiger Beat* would pay a fortune for a picture of Shane in that pose, but she wouldn't be the one to provide it. Over the past few months, the members of YB2 had reached an unwritten agreement—no matter how anxious the entire civilized world was to know their private business, YB2 team members would guard each others' privacy. They were a family, and family members did not leak stories or share pictures of each other.

She was about to return to her reading—a novel by Ray Bradbury, one of her favorite novelists—when a slight movement caught her eye. RC was walking hastily back to the bus with two bulging grocery bags in his hands.

She lifted her head when the door opened with a hydraulic hiss.

"Hey," RC said, climbing the steps. He dropped one grocery bag on the seat next to Paige, then pulled a magazine from the other. "The new *People* is out. Thought you might want to take a look."

Grinning, he moved through the bus, tossing glossy copies onto each band member's seat. Shane woke when the magazine fell into his lap, and Liane found herself holding a copy a moment later.

There on the cover, in living color, she and her friends looked out on the world. The photographer had included Taz and RC in the shot, too, and for once all of them looked good. *On the Road with YB2,* the headline read. *See what the fuss is all about.*

On a wave of excitement, she flipped the pages, searching for a familiar face. There! A shot of Shane and Paige, and another of Josiah and Taz at the soundboard. Turning back to the beginning of the article, she scanned the page to determine how Huck Phillips had set up the story.

She saw four paragraphs of introduction, then subheads introducing each group member, beginning with Shane. A wry smile lifted her mouth. That made sense—every girl in America seemed to be in love with him, so why not lead off with the group's famous hunk?

A short blurb on Paige followed, then a few paragraphs on Noah.

Her heart did a double beat when she saw her own name in bold print: *Liane Nelson, Minneapolis, Minnesota*. Her eyes flew over the paragraphs below the title:

By far the most surprising member of the group is Liane Nelson, from Minneapolis. In her second year with YB2, Liane exudes more polish and intellect at fourteen than most college seniors at graduation. While the other kids sleep and play cards on the bus, Liane stares at the night sky through the window and explains ideas about the origin of the universe. Discussing quarks and black holes as easily as other girls discuss boys and hairstyles, Liane is a college professor in a fourteen-year-old's thin frame—a walking wonder.

She's savvy and intuitive, and yes, a bit cynical. But she laughs with her friends and, when required, plays the role of teenage girl with abandon and glee. Just don't try to sit next to her on the bus when she's window-gazing. Life on the road is "exhausting," she says, and the singers "need space." With an air of diva-ness that could outrival Mariah Carey, she turns away from casual encounters in order to pursue her own lofty thoughts.

She looks like the girl next door, but don't let the strong voice and the agile limbs fool you—this is no flavor-of-the-month singer. Liane Nelson is a brain in flesh, a young Einstein in designer jeans.

Nobel Prize committee—take notice. Maybe you can catch up with her in about ten years . . . if she's in the mood to talk to you.

A ball of heat churned in her stomach as Liane lowered the page. For a moment her mind went blank, then a thousand objections flew through her brain like crows in flight. Hey—this wasn't fair! This man had tricked her! He wasn't supposed to be interviewing her the night he sat in the bus seat and listened to her ramble! He had made her sound like the worst kind of snob, when in reality she had been pleasant but firm.

And he hadn't said anything about their conversation from the next morning, when he had gathered everybody around for the official interview. He had asked Shane about his love for music, he had asked Josiah how it felt to be the new kid in the group, and he had asked her about life in Minneapolis and if she enjoyed shopping at the Mall of America. He had *not* asked her about stars or quarks or the origin of the universe—all that stuff was supposed to be off-limits! He was supposed to be *bored,* not taking mental notes!

She shuddered. This was terrible—awful! Just last month she'd been reading the message boards at the YB2 Web site and someone had remarked that she looked blah ordinary, like a geek . . . now they'd for sure think she was one, and a snob, too! Kids would be drawing pocket protectors on her shirt in the YB2 posters, and they'd sketch Coke-bottle glasses on the end of her nose in publicity pictures. Other kids would think she was some kind of freak. The fans who *did* like her would change their tune in a hurry, and those who had *never* liked her would say, "I *knew* there was something funny about that girl. . . ."

Gulping back tears, she grabbed the magazine and ran to the bathroom, the only spot on the bus where a young Einstein could sit alone and have a good cry.

8

Noah accepted a copy of the magazine from RC, thumbed through it long enough to grin at his picture, then tossed it onto the bunk. He didn't need to read the article and he didn't particularly want to.

He *wanted* to write a song. For four days he'd been trying to write, and so far he had only two things— a G chord and the first line: "There once lived a dog, a very fine dog."

Now he knew what people meant by writer's block. The first chord had been a cinch—he always played in the key of G—and the first line had popped into his head in a flash of inspiration.

After that, he hit a roadblock.

It wasn't for lack of trying. For the last four days he'd spent every spare minute with his guitar in his lap and a thoughtful look on his face. The others had teased him for a while, but when they saw his determination, they left him alone. After all, they all knew songwriting was serious business, *important* business, and Shane and Paige regularly needed time to think and improvise. You couldn't force creative juices—they needed time and space to bubble up.

He'd been waiting for hours.

He was still waiting for the bubbles when Liane rushed by, her face blotchy and her hands curled around the *People* magazine. He put out a hand to stop her, but she went into the bathroom and locked the door.

A moment later, he heard sobs.

So—there was no joy in Mudville, because Liane was upset now too. He couldn't imagine what it was— there'd been no new mail lately—but perhaps she'd used RC's cell phone to call home and heard bad news in the process.

The creative bubbles could wait. He slid his guitar onto the bunk, then stood and rapped on the bathroom door. "Lee? You okay in there?"

After a long moment, the door opened a crack. She blew her nose, then looked at him through puffy eyes. "You need the bathroom?"

"No—I just wanted to see if you were okay."

The door opened wider, then Liane sniffed. "It's this." She thrust the magazine toward him. "That Phillips guy cheated. On that first night when everyone was sleeping, he tried to interview me. So I told him I was tired and didn't want to talk business, and he said okay. So I talked

Liane

about the stars and stuff, and he seemed to be barely interested—in fact, I was trying to put him to sleep. But apparently he remembered enough of what I said because in this article he's made me look like some kind of alien— and a snotty alien, at that!"

Noah pried the magazine from her stiff fingertips. "I haven't read it. What'd he say?"

She stared at him, her eyes round. "You didn't read it?"

"What did he say?"

She crossed her arms and shot an angry look down the aisle. "He said I was more like a college professor than a kid. He said I was a walking brain. He said I was like Einstein when everyone knows I'm not! He said I acted more like a diva than Mariah Carey, and I have *never* tried to act like a superstar—"

Noah put out a hand. "Easy, Lee, calm down. It can't be that bad."

She glared at him from beneath her bangs. "Can't it?"

"Well . . . no. And you *are* smart. I don't see why you wouldn't want the world to know that. I wish I had your brains."

She frowned. "Being smart is okay, Noah, but being a walking brain is just weird. RC wants kids to be able to relate to us, but how is anybody supposed to relate to the weirdo described in that article?"

Noah considered a moment. "I relate to you fine."

"But you know the real me. That article didn't say anything about what I'm really like—he only mentioned quarks and black holes."

"But the real you understands those things. And his article was supposed to be about the real YB2—"

"I don't want people to *know* I understand those things."

Noah frowned at her. Would he ever understand females? Sometimes his mother said contradictory things like this—statements that made no sense at all.

A line appeared between Liane's brows. "Let me put it to you this way—do you want everyone to know everything about you?"

He shrugged. "I don't have anything to hide."

"Oh yeah? Then how would you feel if that reporter had written that you spent a night crying in the bathroom because your dog died?"

For a moment Noah's mind when blank, then panic slipped into the empty space. He flipped the magazine open, searching for the page with his picture. "He didn't write that, did he?"

"I thought you didn't have anything to hide."

"I don't—but it's just that—well, some things are personal."

"Right—some things are. *Now* do you understand why I don't want the world to know I like to think about quarks and the expanding universe?"

He nodded as understanding dawned. "Oh. Yeah, I guess I'm down with that."

She sank onto the edge of a bunk as a glum expression settled on her face. "That magazine is on the newsstands now—within a few days the story will be all over the place. People are never going to think of me in the same way again. When we hold press conferences, reporters will be asking me to solve algebraic equations and do math in my head. Kids who once thought I was cool will think I'm . . . odd. And everyone will think I'm stuck-up." She sniffed. "My mom's gonna kill me. She's always telling me I need to be more friendly with people."

Noah playfully punched her in the arm. "I've always thought you were a little odd, Lee. You've always thought I was goofy. But that's okay."

She made a face at him. "It's different with us."

"Why is it different?"

"It just is." She propped her elbow on her knee, then parked her chin in her palm. "I've got to come up with a way to undo the damage."

Noah lifted a brow. "Can you do that?"

"Of course I can. According to *People* magazine, I'm a bloomin' genius."

9

Ten minutes before their pre-concert call time, Liane sat in the dressing room with a yellow legal pad in her lap. Paige had already gone out to join the others, who were relaxing in the greenroom, but Liane wanted to make the most of her last free minutes.

She had always believed in the value of a good plan. She'd been carrying the legal pad all day, jotting down ideas as they occurred to her.

Already she had tossed one big idea. At the top of her list she had written:

Complain about Huck Phillips and his interviewing techniques.

Then she had drawn a big *X* next to the idea. If she complained, she'd become one of hundreds, even thousands, of people who said too much in interviews and then griped about it. Complaining was neither unique nor effective. If Phillips mentioned her complaint in the magazine, her strategy might prove counter-productive.

Next on her list was:

Dispute Phillips's perceptions in another article.

That idea held promise. Some people believed everything they read in print. If they read Phillips's article last week, they could read another one next week and change their mind. Phillips had made her come across as an academic snot-face; someone else could write that she was a lively, average, all-American girl. Why not?

She moved her pencil to the line beneath her last suggestion and wrote:

Avenues of Action:
1. E-mail or call editors of other magazines and promise an exclusive interview. Consider *CosmoGirl*, *Teen Vogue*, *Tiger Beat*, *Seventeen*, and *Elle Girl*.

She chewed on the end of her pencil. If these editors wanted to interview her, how should they contact her? She could always give them her e-mail address, but a direct contact seemed unprofessional coming from a well-known group like YB2. They'd expect her to have a professional publicity person . . . which she did, sort of.

Aunt Rhonda handled all the publicity for YB2, and surely that included Liane.

Tonight, from the hotel's Internet connection, she could send her e-mails offering an interview. . . and wait.

She kept writing:

2. Ask interested parties to contact publicist/office manager Rhonda Clawson at Orlando office to set up interviews.
3. Wait for responses.
4. Give interviews after appointments have been set up.
5. During interviews, talk about boys, clothes, fashion, and Ashton Kutcher. Giggle a lot. Try to say one thing that could be taken as silly. Be VERY friendly.
6. Remember: never, ever talk about academic subjects around reporters again!

There. She held the legal pad at arm's length and smiled at her plan. This should take care of her public perception problem. Within a month, everyone would have forgotten all about Huck Phillips and his rotten article. She might attract an entirely new set of fans, who could say? Aunt Rhonda and RC would be happy because anything that was good for one team member would be good for the entire team. Extra publicity for her would mean extra publicity for everybody, and people in show business were always saying a group could never have too much of that.

Feeling happier and more relieved than she had in days, Liane tucked the legal pad into her makeup case, then lifted her chin and went out to join the others.

10

One problem with living on the bus, Noah realized, was a serious lack of privacy. After completing his school-work, he was in the front seats strumming his guitar and waiting for inspiration when Josiah stopped in the aisle and looked at the spiral notebook propped against Noah's knees.

Josiah saw the nearly blank page before Noah could snatch it up. "Whatcha doin'?"

"Nothing."

"Looks like something to me."

Peering over his shoulder, Noah studied him. Josiah had proven to be an okay guy. They roomed together when the band regrouped at the house in Orlando, and last month Josiah had trusted Noah enough to tell him about the scoliosis brace he wore under his clothes.

Maybe Noah could confide in him, too.

After glancing around to be sure none of the others was listening, Noah folded his hands atop the guitar. "I'm trying to write a song."

"That much is obvious." Josiah perched on the armrest of the empty seat across the aisle. "You've been playing that same chord all week."

"Not that long." Noah forced a laugh, then lowered his voice. "See, Liane suggested that I write a song about my dog. Trouble is, it's not as easy as you might think. I'm beginning to really appreciate Shane and Paige."

Josiah ripped the top off the box of Cracker Jacks in his hand. He lifted a brow. "Want some?"

Noah shook his head. "Don't want to get my fingers sticky."

Nodding, Josiah poured a handful of caramel popcorn into his palm, then shoveled it into his mouth. Forcing words through a mouthful of popped corn, Josiah said, "Whaft sfo hardf abouf it?"

"I dunno. I've got this little chord thing—a G chord to a C chord, then to a D7—and I've got the first sentence. But after that, man, I just don't know what to do."

Josiah's mouth spread into a caramel-coated smile. "I know."

"You know *what?*"

"I know how to do it. I think you've got it backward. I was reading a music magazine the other day, and it said that most songwriters write the words first. Once you've got the words, then you set the music to it. Much easier that way."

Noah thought a moment, then lowered his guitar. Maybe the guy had a point.

After propping the guitar in the empty seat against the window, Noah picked up his notebook and pencil. He glanced around to be sure no one else was eavesdropping, then leaned his elbow on the armrest and looked up at Josiah. "Want to help?"

"Sure!"

"Okay. I have the first line: 'There once lived a dog, a very fine dog.'" He tilted his head. "Whaddya think?"

Josiah shrugged. "Sounds good to me. Now you write another line, then the next line rhymes with the last word of the first line. What rhymes with *dog?*"

Noah scratched his chin. "Hog. Slog. Trog. Fog. Bog."

"Frog." Josiah poured more Cracker Jacks into his hand. "Pollywog."

Noah made a face. "Pollywog?"

"Why not? It doesn't have to make sense, it only has to rhyme."

"Of course it has to make sense! People don't sing songs that don't make sense."

"Haven't you ever sung 'John Jacob Jingleheimerschmidt'? That song makes no sense at all. Neither does anything with 'shoop shoop' in it, or that stupid thing where you sing, 'Noah, Noah, bo-bo-ah, banana fanna, fo-fo-ah, mee mi, mo-moe-ah—'"

"I get the point. But I want these words to make sense." He lowered his voice. "My song is about Justus, the best dog who ever lived. So it has to be special, and it has to say everything I want to say. This song is all I'll have to remember him by."

Josiah's smile dimmed a degree. "Oh. So—what's your first line again?"

"There once lived a dog, a very fine dog."

Josiah tossed another handful of popcorn into his mouth, chewed a moment, then swallowed. "Okay. What was fine about him?"

"Well . . ." Noah considered. How do you describe your best friend in just a few words? "He was loyal. And nice. And he never met anybody he didn't like."

Josiah continued chewing with a thoughtful look in his eyes. "There once was a dog, a very fine dog. As nice a dog as you could ever meet. He never got pushy, and he loved pollywogs . . . and he loved to eat supersweet treats." He flashed a smile. "Whaddya think?"

Noah grunted as he scratched the words in his notebook. "Give me a minute; let me get it all down."

"I think it'll be easier once you get the rhyme," Josiah added, sliding off the armrest into the seat. "I'll help you—I've always liked poetry. I was pretty good in English at my school."

"Good—'cause I wasn't. Now, what was that second line again?"

"It's just a start; we might have to tweak it a little."

"That's okay—I need to get the thing started. Go on, tell me again. Tell me anything."

Josiah leaned into the aisle and repeated the lines as Noah scratched out the words as best he could.

11

Liane had just slid into a booth at a nearly deserted truck stop somewhere in the middle of an Arizona desert when RC walked over and handed her the cell phone. "Rhonda needs to talk to you."

Glancing at Paige, who had lifted both brows at this announcement, Liane accepted the phone. Rhonda Clawson, RC's sister and the group's publicist and office manager, didn't usually ask to speak to any of the singers when they were on the road . . . unless she had to deliver bad news. A flurry of possibilities flew through Liane's mind—her parents were sick, a relative had died . . .

When she said hello, her voice quivered.

"Liane? How are you, honey?"

Liane looked at Shane, who sat across the table next to Paige. "I'm fine, Aunt Ro. How are things back at the office?"

"They're good. But, hon, I've got to ask—did you send e-mails to several magazines and offer them a personal interview?"

Liane transferred her gaze to the dusty window at her left. The tone of Aunt Rhonda's voice set alarm bells ringing in her head.

"Um . . . yes. Why? Did someone respond?"

"Someone?" Aunt Rhonda laughed, but there was no humor in her voice. "Liane, I've done nothing but answer questions for the last twenty-four hours." She hesitated a moment. "May I ask *why* you contacted them? Ron usually leaves the scheduling of interviews to me. That's my job, you know."

Liane looked at the table as her face began to burn. She hadn't expected her best plan to blow up in her face. She would have to resort to Plan B, but first she would have to get out of this mess.

"I'm sorry, Aunt Rhonda. I didn't mean to make any trouble for you. I thought it would be cool—you know, a few girls' magazines interviewing the girls of YB2. Everyone always wants to interview the entire group, but since Paige and I are the only girls—"

"They aren't asking for Paige. They said you promised them an interview with *you*."

Liane cringed as guilt avalanched over her. The idea had seemed flawless when she first thought of it, but something had gone horribly wrong. She was coming off as a snob again, and that wasn't at all the picture she wanted to present, especially not to Aunt Rhonda.

"Why, Lee?" Aunt Rhonda's voice was soft and insistent. "Why the urgent need to talk to all these people?"

Liane shut her eyes against a rush of tears, uncomfortably aware that the table conversation between Shane, Paige, and Taz had suddenly stopped. They had to know something was up, and in a minute they'd be asking what was wrong.

How could she explain that she'd tried to grab the spotlight for really *good* reasons?

Aunt Rhonda persisted. "I've been thinking, Lee, and I think I've got a pretty good handle on what's troubling you. Did that *People* article upset you?"

Unable to speak, Liane nodded, then realized Aunt Rhonda couldn't see her. "Uh-huh."

"Oh, honey." Rhonda's voice filled with sympathy. "When will you realize that being smart is nothing to be ashamed of? You're a wonderful, bright young woman, and everybody loves you. You don't have to prove yourself to anyone, especially not these magazines."

Liane nodded, then sniffled into the phone. Shane and Taz lifted their menus and pretended to study them while Paige quietly turned her head toward the warmth of the sunlit window.

"Are you okay?" Aunt Rhonda's voice whispered in Liane's ear.

"Um . . . yeah."

"Okay, then. Let me call these editors back and suggest that they postpone their stories until later, when you and Paige may be able to give an interview together.

And from now on, let me handle the publicity, okay? Between performing and your schoolwork, you have enough pressure in your life."

Liane forced the word through her thick throat: "Okay."

"Is RC close by?"

"He's at the next table."

"Would you give the phone to him, please?"

Liane cleared her throat as she waved the cell phone over Taz's shoulders. "RC? Aunt Rhonda wants to talk to you."

After he took the phone and moved back to his booth, Liane picked up her menu and stared at the words behind yellowed plastic. What had she been thinking? She *hadn't* been thinking, that was the problem. She had never meant to step out-of-bounds, but no one had explained exactly what the publicity boundaries were. Still, she had let fame go to her head, hoping—no, *knowing*—that magazine people would want to talk to her. Everybody wanted a piece of YB2, and no one had ever gotten an exclusive interview with any of the singers.

She'd taken a bad problem and made it far worse.

And she'd forgotten one big thing: RC always stressed that they were a team and that individual fame wasn't important. They were supposed to work together in almost everything, and fame was the least of their motivations. They were trying to spread a message, but the only message she had wanted to spread was about herself . . . how snobby was *that*?

So her idea about gaining more publicity was a loser.

As soon as she stopped feeling stupid and ashamed, she'd scratch it off her legal pad and come up with another idea.

She knew she could be inventive when she set her mind to something. She'd have to come up with another way to correct the way America thought of her. Within a few days, she was sure to think of something.

She had just given her order to the middle-aged waitress when the woman's eyes widened to the size of dinner plates. "Wait a minute!" She whirled to look at the other table, then spun back around to the table where Liane was sitting. "You're *them!* Those kids! That XYZ group!"

"It's YB2," Taz said, nodding politely. "But yes, that's us."

"Well . . . isn't that enough to fry your grits! Running into you guys, right here in Bubba's diner." Her smile broadened. "Why, I was just reading about you all. Somebody left one of those teen magazines in the girls' bathroom, and I pulled it out when I needed something to read on my break. Hang on a minute—would you all autograph it for me?"

Liane managed a weak smile, but the others laughed and said it'd be no trouble. As the waitress hurried away, Liane leaned forward to whisper to her friends. "I'm not sure you even want to touch something that's been in the bathroom. Do you have any idea how many germs there could be on that paper? Stuff aerosolizes in bathrooms, you know."

"What kind of stuff?" Paige asked.

Liane crinkled her nose. "Bad stuff. Germy stuff. Stuff you don't want to talk about at the dinner table. And when it turns into tiny water vapor droplets, it settles on whatever's in the room. But you guys don't care, and you're going to hold that magazine right in your hands and sign it on the same table that's going to hold our food—" She closed her eyes and shuddered. "I'm going to have to go wash my hands after this."

"Well, watch out for the bad stuff around the sink," Shane said, grinning. "Face it, Liane. If germs are gonna get you, they're gonna get you. Why worry about them?"

She was about to reply when the waitress breezed over, a copy of a tattered magazine in her hand. Liane recognized the title from ten feet away—*Tiger Beat,* the teenage version of *Soap Opera Digest.* Except that in *Tiger Beat,* the stars were members of young bands and life itself was the soap opera.

Her jaw dropped when she saw her own picture, huge and in living color, in a highlighted square on the cover. "Liane of YB2," the caption read. "Is she hot? Or just a snot?"

The waitress handed the magazine to Shane. "There's a picture of your entire group on the cover and inside," she said, beaming. "Would you sign in both places?"

"Wait—gimme that." Liane leaned across the table and jerked the magazine from Shane's hand. In a few frantic flips she had located the cover story, this time with the title: "Liane Acting Like a Diva? Fans Say: Leave-ah!"

She drew an agonized breath.

"What's wrong?" Paige asked. "Is the bad stuff getting to you already?"

Liane couldn't speak. Holding the slick pages in trembling fists, she mumbled her way through the first paragraph: "Since published reports of Liane Nelson's snobbery and diva-like behavior surfaced last week, fans of YB2 have revolted in numbers. Somewhere an Internet petition to remove her from the group is circulating, while more creative fans have created 'Snub the Snob' Web pages. They are suggesting that director Ron Clawson replace Liane with a younger version of Britney Spears or Avril Lavigne. For the record, this reporter has never met the ultra-intelligent Liane . . . but perhaps that's because she 'needs her space.'"

"Arrrrrgh!" Dropping the magazine, Liane let her head fall back.

Shane took the magazine and skimmed through the article, then pulled a pen from his pocket. "Cheer up, Lee, it's not that bad," he said, signing his name across his picture. "It's not like anybody really believes this stuff."

"I don't believe it," the waitress said, the crack of her gum accenting her words. "You look like a right nice young lady to me. And I don't even know who that April person is."

"Avril," Paige corrected. "She's very big."

"Not around here," the waitress replied, sliding the magazine toward Liane. "Just sign right here, hon, on your big cover picture. I think I'm going to frame this and put it behind the counter."

Clutching her hand to her stomach, Liane caught Taz's eye. "I think I'm going to be sick."

The waitress laughed. "Just wait until after you eat Bubba's cookin'."

12

Noah waited until everyone settled back into
their places and Larry put the engine into gear. When the
bus nosed its way back onto the highway, Noah grabbed
his notebook and walked to the front where Liane sat
alone in a seat. She had turned her face to the window
and wore a gloomy expression . . . well, that was okay.
His song would cheer her up.

"Hey." He sank into the seat next to her.

The look she gave him wasn't exactly welcoming, but
he pressed on. "I was wondering—well, I took your advice
and started writing a song. But I couldn't get the ball
rolling, so Josiah suggested I write the words first, then
put them to music."

A faint smile flitted across her lips. "You and Joe
wrote lyrics together?"

"Well . . . I don't know if they're lyrics, exactly;

it looks more like a poem on paper. But when we sing it, it'll be better, I know. I mean, half the songs in the world look goofy on paper, but they sound cool when you add the music."

Liane extended her hand in a dramatic flourish. "Let me see it, then."

He felt the tips of his ears burn as he handed her the notebook. She took it, scanned the page, then focused on the first line: "There once lived a dog, a very fine dog."

"Shhh!" Noah sank lower in his seat. "Can't you read it silently? I don't want the others to hear anything until it's all done."

She gave him the look his mother always gave him when she'd caught him sneaking scraps of food under the table for Justus. "You're never going to get a sense of the rhythm until you read it aloud. Poetry is more than rhyme and words—it's meter, too."

"What?"

"Remember? Meter is the rhythm of the sound. Most people count out the syllables to make sure they match."

"Oh yeah." Grinning sheepishly, Noah leaned his head on his hand. "We didn't count anything."

Liane looked back at the page. "Well, maybe you got lucky. If the lines are about the same length, you might have hit on the right meter."

Noah didn't think so, but he decided to let her make up her mind for herself.

Speaking in a low, quiet voice, Liane began to read:

"There once lived a dog, a very fine dog,
He was as nice a dog as you could meet.
He liked everyone he met in the bog,
And he especially liked his doggie treats."

She looked at Noah. "He lived in a *bog?* What in the world are you talking about?"

"We had to find something that rhymed with *dog*. It was either *bog* or *pollywog*."

She shook her head. "Let's keep going."

"This dog was mine, a special friend,
He lived with me five years.
I thought he'd live with me until the end,
And so I'm crying buckets of tears."

She didn't comment on the second verse, and Noah couldn't see her face as she hung her head. He tried to peek beneath the curtain of her hair, then decided it'd be best to wait. If she was laughing . . . well, maybe he didn't want to see that.

"Justus was a great, big dog,
He loved to eat his treats.
He had black ears that dragged on logs—
And he had great big doggie feet.
He flew in an airplane, he swam in the pool,
He slept by my bed and snored all night.
He even went with me to my school,
When I was sad, he made things all right."

Liane caught her breath and pressed her hand to her lips—for a moment, Noah was certain he had made her cry. This was a song about a dead dog, so it was bound to be sad, right? He wanted people to feel stuff, and if Liane was crying, the poem must be awfully good.

"I miss my dog," she read, a crack in her voice, "my very fine dog,
    The nicest dog as you could ever meet.
    And if you meet a big dog in the fog,
    I hope you'll give him a nice doggie treat."

Liane lowered the notebook, then pressed both hands to her face. Silence wrapped around them like a blanket.

Was she crying? Noah nudged her with his elbow. "Um, Joe helped me with the spelling. There's no way I could have written anything that good all by myself."

Noah felt heat flush his body from head to toe when Liane sobbed. He was about to congratulate himself for writing such a moving tribute to Justus, but then she tipped her head back and howled. She wasn't crying. She was *laughing*—shrieking loud enough to wake a coma patient. Tears streamed down her cheeks and smeared her makeup while her fists pounded the notebook in her lap.

Noah snatched the book to his chest. "Good grief! It's not that funny!"

"It's—it's hysterical!"

"See if I ever show you anything again!"

"Hey." From where she sat at the tables, Paige lifted her head. "What's so funny up there?"

"Nothing!" Noah stood, about to stomp to the back of the bus, but Liane grabbed the bottom of his shirt. "Don't go. I'm sorry, I didn't mean to hurt your feelings. It's—well, it's so *you*, Noah. It's funny, that's all."

He rolled his eyes. "For once in my life, I wasn't trying to be funny."

"I know." She took a deep breath. "I'm sorry, I didn't mean to make fun of it. It's just not what I expected. You were so upset over Justus, that's why I didn't expect something funny. But I've gotta thank you—I was feeling so bad I didn't know if I'd ever laugh again."

Noah slid back into the seat to acknowledge defeat, then looked at Liane and grinned. "Man, I just don't know how to do this." He lifted a brow. "You told me it'd be easy."

"I didn't say it'd be easy—I said you could do it. And I still think you can, but you need to do it a little differently."

"Write the music first?"

"No—stick with the lyrics; they're the skeleton your tune will hang on. But think about this—you tried to write about Justus, but will a song about him ever mean as much to other people as it does to you?"

He propped his chin on his hand. "Um . . . probably not."

"Right. And if you want your words to touch someone, they have to be about feelings everyone has. Lots of people lose pets they love—and they lose family members, too. And if you write a song about your loss, you'll reach more people and really touch their heart. And then—" she pointed at him—"if you write about how you found comfort when you were sad, you'll help others."

He shook his head. "I don't see how all that fits into a song about Justus. And . . . well, I was hoping to feel better after writing the song. I still miss him something awful."

"Of course you do. And the song won't be about Justus, exactly, but about what you felt when you lost him. As you figure out what you want to say, you might stumble across the feeling you're looking for. And by helping other people deal with their own hurts, you'll be honoring Justus's memory. See how it works?"

The pieces began to fall into place as he looked at her. Liane was smart; when other people were focusing on stupid little details, she always saw the big picture. Justus had been a dog, only a dog, but if Noah could do what she said, Justus could become a hero, even after his death.

He gripped his notebook. "I'll try it again."

"Good. Don't worry so much about the rhyme this time. Just let whatever's in your heart flow out." She grinned at him. "You can always fix the spelling and stuff later."

Buoyed by a kind of confidence he hadn't felt in a long time, Noah tucked his notebook under his arm and went in search of a quiet place to work.

13

Thursday, September 9

Liane hummed a snatch of melody as she pinned
her new earrings to her pierced ears. She'd never worn
anything like these before—the sparkly chains dangled
almost to her shoulders, and they were sure to dazzle in
the stage lights. The clerk at the Home Shopping Clear-
ance center had assured her they were *cool,* and Liane
had been looking for something to update her look.

Last month, after hearing herself described as "blah
ordinary" on a YB2 Internet message board, she'd tried
several things to spruce up her looks: green streaked
hair, charm bracelets, glittery makeup. Shane had
reminded her that a person's outside appearance didn't
change a thing about who they were *inside,* and she was
cool with that. These earrings weren't going to change
who she was on the inside, but her coolness quotient
needed an uplift, and fast. Earrings alone wouldn't do it,

Liane

but earrings, a new attitude, and a public relations counterattack might.

She fastened the back on the last earring, then stepped back and nodded her head, admiring her reflection in the mirror. These would look *good,* especially when they sparkled onstage as she danced.

So changing the outward appearance didn't do a thing about the inward person. Fine. Trouble was, the public never really got to know celebrities as real people. She'd had several opportunities to meet movie stars and famous singers since joining YB2, and she'd had some real surprises. Some of the hippest actors were ignorant doofheads in person, and one of the most beautiful movie stars in the world had shown up at one gig with dirty feet and chipped fingernails. Liane had been even more shocked to learn that this famous woman, who looked smart and classy on-screen, couldn't ask for a bottle of water without cussing.

RC was always saying that he never wanted the singers of YB2 to be seen as anything less than wholesome American teenagers. . . . Of course, he always had high expectations of them, even when no one was looking. But whenever anyone outside the group was within listening distance, they were to be especially professional and keep YB2's image in mind. This image was supposed to be fun and friendly, not brainy or rude, so Liane still had to do something to correct the impressions left by the articles in *People* and *Tiger Beat*.

She looked at her watch—two minutes before call

time, and Paige had already stepped into the hallway to meet the guys. They had dressed early tonight because they were supposed to meet a local DJ broadcasting from the civic center's parking lot. An entire squadron of security guards waited to escort them through the parking lot to the RV serving as a mobile studio, so she couldn't be late.

After another quick check in the mirror, Liane smeared her lips with a coat of lip gloss, then slipped the container into her sleeve and buttoned the cuff. When a girl couldn't carry a purse, sometimes a sleeve worked just as well.

Noah, Josiah, Shane, and Paige were already standing in the hall when she stepped out of the dressing room. RC gave her the briefest glance, then pointed to the loading dock. "That's the way out, where the security guards will meet you. I've got to go see Taz about an AV problem, but Shane will take you over."

Liane and the others fell into step beside Shane as he led the way out. No matter how many times they performed at a huge arena, she was always a little amazed to realize that over twenty thousand people would come to hear them sing tonight. Their bus had driven through good-sized *towns* of fewer people than that.

"Hey, Lee." Shane thumped her on the back. "What's that you've got hanging from your ears?"

"What's it look like?"

"Sparkly pumpkins."

"Then maybe that's what they are."

She'd hoped their group could make it to the RV before anyone noticed them, but some fans were hard to slip past. As soon as they stepped from the loading dock into the sunshine, someone outside the fence screamed, "There they are! Shane! Noah!" and the race began. The security guards who walked outside their little group were all burly men, but even they seemed surprised by the hubbub and the rush toward YB2.

Liane breathed a sigh of relief when they spotted the RV emblazoned with the radio station's call letters. The DJ had parked no more than fifty yards from the loading dock, but the distance was enough to leave Liane feeling winded . . . and enough to give the fans a taste of genuine excitement.

"Hello, YB2!" The heavy, bearded guy behind the soundboard gave them a thumbs-up as they filled the available space inside the crowded RV. A red ON AIR light on the desk warned them not to talk. Besides, the DJ was doing enough talking for all of them.

"You'll never believe who just walked through my door," he said, leaning closer to the microphone on the desk. "YB2, every one of them! Shane, Paige, Josiah, Liane, and Noah! And I'm here to tell you they're just as fine-looking in person as they are on TV!"

He chattered a bit more, then clicked a button. The ON AIR light was now off, and Liane heard strains of "Y B Alone?" through the speakers, then the DJ leaned back in his chair and grinned at them.

"Hey, guys," he said, speaking in a flatter and more

Liane

nasal voice than he'd used a moment ago. "We've only got about three minutes between songs, so I'm going to do little spot interviews with each of you, okay?" He looked at Shane. "And we really appreciate you letting us come out here. Our ratings have been up all week."

"That's fine." Shane looked at the group. "You guys just relax for a minute, okay? I'll go first. We'll make this quick, then we'll go inside and get ready for the concert."

Liane put her hands behind her back and leaned against the wall. Had the DJ noticed her new earrings? Surely he'd realize that only a really cool girl would dangle shining tangerines from long chains attached to her ears. These were definitely not Einstein earrings, not at all something a geek would wear.

She tossed her head and caught Noah's eye. His eyes twinkled above a devilish smile, and she had the feeling he knew exactly what she was trying to do.

She looked away before he could say something she'd regret.

When the song ended, the DJ leaned into his mike, clicked on a button, and pointed at Shane. "You'll never believe who I have sitting across from me," he said, his voice low and breathy again. "That heartthrob of the tweenage set, the boy all American moms wish they could call 'son.' Shane Clawson, himself! How are ya, Shane?"

Shane leaned into the hanging mike. "I'm good, thanks."

"How are you enjoying your time in Dallas? You had a chance to see many of the sights?"

"Oh, it's great—we love it." Shane grinned at Liane, who rolled her eyes. Maybe the town was beautiful, but all they'd seen of it was their hotel and the civic center.

"That's good. Well, we're glad to have you in our fair city. Hey, Noah—how ya doin', dude? You're the California surfer boy, aren't you?"

Noah leaned past Paige into the mike. "Um, yeah. I'm from San Diego, and I love surfing. Don't get to catch many waves on the road, though."

"I can dig it. And Paige Clawson—tell me, do you really write most of the group's songs?"

Paige waited as Shane silently maneuvered her chin toward the microphone. "Well . . . yes, but I have a lot of help. My brother helps with the lyrics, and my dad writes most of the music. We like to think of ourselves as a team."

"And a winning team you are. Congratulations on a job well done."

Liane froze when the DJ's eyes turned toward her. "Liane Nelson! Step up here and let me talk atcha."

She forced a polite smile as she shuffled between Noah and Paige.

"Hey, Liane—" the guy drummed on the tabletop— "I hear you're a walking genius. What's the square root of 144?"

Anybody past eighth grade would have known the answer, but Liane was in no mood to perform like a trained monkey. She stared at the man a moment, deciding on her strategy, then she drew a deep breath, leaned into the mike . . . and giggled.

No one spoke. Even the DJ dropped his jaw as the room filled with dead air . . . the worst thing that can happen on radio.

"Um . . .uh—" the DJ stammered as he forced words across his tongue—"don't you *know* the square root of 144?"

She shook her head until her earrings danced, and let out another giggle.

The DJ cast a helpless look at Shane. "Ohhhh-kaaaay. I see we're not going anywhere with that question, so let me play another song. Take it away, YB2!"

As the strains of "Never Stop Believin'" filled the RV, Liane backed away from the mike. Shane was glaring at her, his eyes narrowed, while Paige was laughing so hard she had to cover her mouth with her hand.

"Good one." Noah nudged her in the ribs as she stepped back. "What are you trying to prove?"

"Absolutely nothing," she whispered.

The DJ gestured toward a black telephone, where several lights were flickering. "We, uh, have some callers on the line, some kids who want to ask you a few questions. You guys okay with that?"

"We're ready," Shane said. "We do this all the time."

"Great." The DJ turned away, tapping his fingers on the desktop as the music played through the speakers. As the last few bars of "Never Stop Believin'" filled the trailer, the DJ leaned into the mike and pushed a button on the telephone. "Hello? You're sharin' the airwaves with YB2! What do you want to ask the group?"

"I want to know—" the voice was high, girlish, and very opinionated—"why Liane hates us fans so much. I read what she said about us in *People*—about how she needs her space and all—and I just wanted to tell her that without us, she'd be a big fat nothing! I'm voting to snub the snob!"

Liane felt her jaw drop as the DJ's eyes swiveled to meet hers. "Liane . . ." he began, a half smile twisting his face, "do you want to reply to that?"

She nodded helplessly, then stepped forward into the empty space created when Noah and Paige cringed away from the mike.

How should she handle this? Plan A, which involved acting silly and simple, no longer seemed like the best approach. She needed to say *something* to this girl, but she had no idea what kind of answer to give.

She tried a compromise approach. "I love our fans," she began, forcing a laugh.

"Oh, no you don't! I read what you told that reporter. He said you were the biggest diva of them all, and—"

"I was misquoted," Liane interrupted. "You can't believe everything you read."

"Oh, yeah? If he lied, why aren't you suing him or something?"

Liane blinked, then threw up her hands and stepped away from the mike. Shane covered for her by leaning toward the mike and thanking the girl for calling. "All of us in YB2 appreciate our fans," he said, smiling at the DJ. "We know we wouldn't be able to do any of the things we do without your support. And I can assure you that Liane is no diva. She's like a sister to me."

He nodded to the DJ, who clicked another button. The girl on the other end of the line wanted to ask Paige where she bought her sunglasses.

Stepping back to the wall, Liane lowered her head and fervently wished the ground would open up and swallow her whole.

14

Liane knew she was in trouble when RC paused longer than usual before speaking. They had gathered in the greenroom, a small room reserved for them in the backstage area of the arena. Everyone sat on sofas except RC, who sat in a chair. Usually before a concert he shared a devotional thought and led them in prayer, but apparently something was weighing on his mind tonight.

Liane suspected she was the cause . . . but she could be wrong. The problem at the soundboard could be stressing him out, and it was entirely possible he hadn't even heard the radio interview.

RC's head swiveled in her direction. "Lee," he asked, his voice as smooth as butter, "what's the square root of 144?"

So he *had* heard.

She lowered her head. "Twelve."

"Ah, yes. Twelve. Did that just come to you?"

Liane shuffled her feet. "No."

No one spoke for a long minute. Liane lifted her eyelids long enough to see that Shane, Noah, and Josiah were looking at the tips of their shoes, probably not wanting to witness her agony. Even Paige had lowered her head, avoiding Liane's embarrassment.

RC finally went on. "Would it have *killed* you to answer the man's question?"

Liane drew a breath. "I guess not."

"Then why didn't you?"

"Because . . ." She hesitated a moment, torn between submission and self-defense. Pride won out. "Because he already knew the answer. He only wanted to make me look like a geek."

RC pressed his lips together. "I'm afraid I have to disagree. If you had answered politely, with the correct answer, you would have told the world that you are a bright and courteous young woman, no more."

He shook his head slightly, opened his hand, then closed it as if he couldn't grasp the words he wanted to say. "I'm not even sure where the word *geek* comes from, but I know I don't like it. It's not kind, it's not uplifting, and I don't want to hear any of you using it about anyone, ever. I especially never want to hear you using it about yourselves."

Liane closed her eyes. Honestly, sometimes RC could be so cool, and other times he could be so . . . paternal.

She could close her eyes and almost hear her dad's voice coming through RC's mouth.

Sighing, RC leaned back in his chair. "You know I love you guys—and I often have to resist the urge to pop a few of these nosy reporters right on the chin. I'd do anything for you . . . and that means correcting you when you need it." He nodded toward Noah. "You ready with our devotion, Noah?"

Noah nodded as he pulled a slip of paper from his pocket. "Yeah. I read this the other day, and I thought it was a good verse."

He smoothed out the paper. "Proverbs 15:14: 'A wise person is hungry for truth, while the fool feeds on trash.'"

Liane stared at the floor. What was *that* supposed to mean? Was Noah calling her a fool . . . or insinuating that she'd been feeding on trash? Shane was the junk food junkie, not her.

"I think," Noah slowly went on, "God is trying to tell us about the difference between being God-smart and human-smart. What do you all think?"

He looked around the circle, waiting for a volunteer, but no one spoke.

"I think," RC said, filling the silence, "what you call 'human-smart' is a person's natural ability to solve problems and remember what he or she learns. Being God-smart, on the other hand, is being able to see things as God does . . . and understanding the difference between what he considers important and what people consider important."

Liane bit her lip, digesting this answer. To her, smart was smart. She'd never really thought about two different kinds of intelligence.

"Yeah," Noah answered. "I mean, the world is filled with smart people—I'm not one of them, but I see them all the time." He grinned as Liane smiled. "I don't see many people who are God-smart, but I think that's easier to get. Even though you might have to be born with a quick brain to be human-smart, the Bible says we can become God-smart if we try—not as smart *as* God, but at least a little like him. Anybody know how?"

Feeling suddenly guilty, Liane kept her eyes focused on the floor. She'd been exercising her brain a lot in the last few days . . . and making a total mess of things.

Josiah lifted his hand in a little wave. "You mean . . . like reading the Bible and stuff?"

Noah nodded. "Yeah. Anybody else?"

Paige lifted her hand. "How about from other people? I've learned a lot by listening to Aunt Rhonda and some of the older people at our church. Whenever a situation comes up and I don't know what to do, I ask them how they'd handle things. They always seem to have good advice."

"Good point, Paige." A smile crept into Noah's voice. "I don't always listen to my elders, but I always *wish* I'd listened after I get busted for messing up."

Liane cringed—was that crack directed at her? She lifted her head and met Noah's eyes. Maybe Noah's entire devotion had her name written all over it. He'd watched her little performance in the radio interview and thrown these thoughts together to teach her a thing or two.

"You can ask God for wisdom," Shane added, stretching out his legs. "There's a place in James that says if we want wisdom, all we have to do is ask God for it."

"That's right, Shane. And Noah, that was a good verse to share." RC leaned forward and propped his elbows on his bent knees. "You kids can grow up and go to college and earn a dozen doctorate degrees, but without wisdom, you'll be educated, not wise. Now I want you guys to be educated, sure. But more than that, I want you to be wise in how you approach life and how you treat other people. This afternoon . . . well, let's just say I heard about a situation that could have benefited from a healthy dose of wisdom."

Though he hadn't called her name, Liane felt the sting in his words. So . . . she'd acted like a fool at the radio interview. Had she really done such a terrible thing? She'd only acted like most other girls her age. Besides, that DJ had baited her, trying to reinforce her image as the all-American nerd, and that nasty caller had left her speechless.

But . . . she still needed to apologize. To keep RC's respect, she had to admit she'd made a mistake.

"I'm sorry, everybody," she said, lifting her head. "I was out of line back at the interview. I didn't mean to do anything stupid, but my attitude got the best of me. And then that awful caller caught me by surprise."

Josiah grinned at her. "I thought you were funny

when you giggled into the mike. What you did was just so . . . not you."

And wasn't that the point? At least Josiah wasn't judging her.

RC cleared his throat, then slapped his hand on his knee. "Okay, then. Are we ready to pray and give another concert?"

The group members rose to their feet, as did RC. Liane followed an instant later, her heart heavy with resentment.

It wasn't fair that she'd gotten a lecture instead of sympathy. How in the world could she make RC understand that she wasn't to blame for causing any of this trouble?

15

Tucked away in the safety of their hotel room, Liane gritted her teeth and tried to ignore the constant smacking of Paige's gum. Paige was sitting in her bed, her headphones over her ears and her laptop in her lap. Like a good student, she was listening to a textbook on tape and trying to finish her weekly lessons.

Liane ignored the tendril of guilt that snaked into her thoughts. She was at the desk tapping on her own laptop. Paige probably thought Liane was hard at work, too, but Liane wasn't connected to the Internet site where they uploaded their homework. No, she was visiting a chat room linked to the YB2 fan site. She'd gone in ten minutes ago and waited for the conversation to become interesting, but the kids online seemed more eager to talk about Shane and Noah than anything else.

Liane

She stared at the blinking cursor in the chat box. Someone named YB2FAN1 was dominating the conversation, and the girl obviously had a serious crush on Shane.

YB2FAN1: omg! Did u c him last nite? ET had pix of shane with noah at the teen choice awards. omg!

GRLNLUV: yes, I saw him. and I thought he was a dog! Well, I'm o1/2k. I've sn him lk btr.

YB2FAN1: The teen choice awards were in LA last month. But I c commercials bout the latin grammys—YB2 rules! they r singing!

MANDASU: lol! kewl! Did u c the new kid? joeziah is his name.

GRLNLUV: Is that how u spell it? jw.

YB2FAN1: I think u spell it joesiah.

Liane couldn't contain herself any longer. As if they had minds of their own, her fingers began flying across the keyboard.

LINDYLU: it's JOSIAH. i m sur.

GRLNLUV: o. thankx.

YB2FAN1: sry. btw, which is your fav YB2 singr?

Liane paused a moment. No one in the world would ever guess that "Lindy Lu" was Liane Nelson, but still . . . was going undercover like this really *honest?* Well . . . it wasn't exactly *dis*honest, and her motivations were okay—she was only doing this to keep in touch with their fans. RC wanted other kids to relate to them, so she had to know what they thought of her so she could make herself relatable.

LINDYLU: My fav YB2-r is liane, i think. what do
           u think of hr?
GRLNLUV: lol!
YB2FAN1:   hlolarawchawmp!
MANDASU: dn't u read what she sd in the mag? She
           is like so snotty. i like page. my fave sngr
           is shane, tho.
GRLNLUV: got 2 go. kit. cya ltr.
MANDASU: ttyl. b4n!

The lines scrolled across the screen as fast as Liane could read them. She understood most of the chat room shorthand, but "hlolarawchawmp" was a puzzle. Tomorrow, she'd have to ask Taz what it meant.

One thing was clear—at least one of these girls was laughing at her while the other hated her.

Summoning her courage, she typed again:

LINDYLU: what's so fnny bout liane?

No one answered for a moment, then:

GRLNLUV: idn. I thot she ws in luv w/shane.
LINDYLU: she's not! lol! Thr jst friends.

YB2FAN1: lian luvs noah.

MANDASU: i thot u had to go?

GRLNLUV: j/k.

LINDYLU: liane does not luv Noah!

YB2FAN1: she lks at him whn they sing. I think ppl no they are n luv.

LINDYLU: they are not n luv!

MANDASU: and how wld u no? i dn care if she luvs shane. i hate hr. relly. I wn go 2 c hr ever. I painted ov hr face n my YB2 pster.

Liane sat back and let her hands fall into her lap. This last girl honestly hated her guts—she had never heard anyone say they had painted over her face in a group poster! How could this girl hate someone she had never met or even tried to understand?

A sense of strangeness settled over Liane—how odd to be thinking of herself as if she were watching her own life, like some creature straight out of the twilight zone.

She attacked the keyboard again.

LINDYLU: I read about liane in a zine. she is nt in luv w anyone now. she luvs singing, tho. n that mag ws wrong. shez really nice.

YB2FAN1: I rd the art in ppl mag. It sad she wuz vry smrt. And if shez smrt, she has 2 luv shane.

MANDASU: I hrd shez a diva. Hrd 2 b leve, tho. YB2 is 2 cool. m/b they will dump hr.

GRLNLUV: maybe thatz y shane does not luv hr. :-)
YB2FAN1: w b alone if she luvs shane? i wood trade
          plcs w her any tme.
MANDASU: ROFLOL!

Liane groaned as the telephone rang, then she looked into the mirror on the wall. In the glass she saw Paige fumble for the phone, then pull out her iPod earbuds and lift the receiver to her ear. "Hello?"

Liane checked her watch. This would be RC's checkup call—every night they were on the road he called the girls' hotel room at eleven to make sure they were safely locked into their room.

"Yes, Dad, we're both here," Paige said, her voice soft and distracted. "We're doing homework. Yes, the door is locked and bolted. No, we're not going out for anything. Yeah. Okay. Love you. See you in the morning."

As she dropped the receiver back into its cradle Paige lifted her head. "Call's at ten tomorrow. We get to sleep in."

Liane blinked at her laptop's scrolling screen. "Okay."

The problem was worse than she thought. Not only did the world think she was a nerdy diva, but they thought her personality was some kind of guy repellant, making Shane and Noah despise her. And while she liked both guys as brothers, she had never been attracted to either of them. One week on the bus had convinced her they were not her idea of Prince Charming, but no one outside the group would understand that. The fans naturally assumed that if she was cool, the group's guys would like her . . . but who could like a teenage freak-genius girl?

Paige pulled the earphones from her neck and yawned. "I'm ready for bed, Lee. You nearly done with your homework?"

Liane gave the computer one last look—YB2FAN1 and GRLNLUV were now arguing over which guy in YB2 had the most beautiful eyes—then clicked her way out of the chat room.

She closed the laptop's lid. "I'm done."

But she wasn't done, not by a long shot. She still had a big-time public perception problem, and she had no idea how to fix it.

16

Noah sat on a pile of luggage outside the hotel and
bent over his notebook. Because the concert last night
had gone off without a hitch and they didn't have far to
travel today, RC had set a late call time—10 A.M., a luxury
for sure. Noah had roomed with Shane in the hotel and
left that sluggard asleep when he left the room at nine
to get some breakfast.

Now Noah sat under the covered driveway and con-
centrated on the blank page. Several uniformed bellhops
had asked if he needed assistance; he had politely told
each of them he just wanted to sit and think. Liane had
given him good advice about how to write his song . . .
trouble was, he still didn't have a clue how this songwriting thing was supposed to work.

He turned his head when the sliding glass doors
of the hotel opened behind him. Paige stepped out,

Liane

navigating with her cane while pulling her rolling suitcase with her free hand. As always, he was amazed at how well she got around.

She lifted her head, seeming to scan the parking lot through her dark glasses, and then her face lit with a smile. "Noah? You out here all by yourself?"

He grinned. "Wow. How'd you know it was me?"

"You're the only guy I know who showers in cologne." She took a step toward him, then paused. "Anywhere to sit out here? I thought I'd come out early and enjoy the sun."

"There's a bench beside the door. Come on, I'll walk you over."

He took her suitcase and set it down next to his, then caught her elbow and walked her to a bench in a patch of dappled sunlight. He sat with her, then crossed his ankle over his knee and looked out at the parking lot.

Paige drew a deep breath, then nodded toward the notebook in his lap. "What's that you're working on?"

He gasped. "How'd you know—"

"I heard the rustle of the paper. And since I know you don't read the newspaper, I figured you had your notebook out again."

Noah rolled his eyes. "I didn't want to tell you. It's embarrassing."

She laughed. "I don't think you need to worry about being embarrassed in front of me. So—what do you have there?"

He thumped the blank page. "I'm trying to write a song about my dog. Justus . . . well, he died, you know."

"I heard. And I'm real sorry about that."

"Thanks." He swallowed the sudden knot that rose in his throat. "Lee said I should write a song, so I tried. I couldn't get anywhere, so Joe helped me write it like a poem. I read the poem to Liane, and she howled because it was completely horrible. She said I shouldn't actually write about Justus, but about all the things I was feeling—you know, stuff other people could relate to. But now I'm stuck. I don't know where to begin."

Paige nodded. "I could help."

"Aw, Paige, I don't want to ask you to help me. You and Shane are so good at this, you're going to think I'm a complete dunce. I'm not good with words."

"You don't have to be good with words, Noah. You have to be good *here*." She lifted her hand and lightly pointed to her heart. "If you *feel* things, if you care, then you can express those feelings in a song. But writing a song without understanding the construction is like trying to build a house without knowing how to read a blueprint or use a hammer. You need to know the basics."

"Yeah? Like what?"

"Well—like knowing the structure of your song. Most songs on the radio today are verse-chorus-verse-chorus-bridge-chorus. Or they could be verse-chorus-verse-chorus. And you need to put the title of the song in the chorus, preferably in the last line."

He stared at her with his mouth slightly open.

"Where'd you learn all this stuff? I thought Lee was smart, but you're a genius, too."

She giggled. "It's not genius, you goof, it's just something my dad taught me. You think Shane and I were born knowing this stuff? No way—Dad taught us. Some of our first songs were pretty hilarious, too. No way anybody would ever want to record them."

"I'll bet mine was funnier." Noah sighed as he thought about his pitiful first effort. "But you said something about the title—what if I don't even have a title?"

"Then get one." Paige's voice was light. "In fact, that's the best place to start. Choose a title that sums up what you want to say in your song, and try to make sure it's unique. Once you have the title, all the other parts sort of fall into place. Oh—and remember to show, not tell. That's a biggie."

Noah made a face. "I have no idea what you're talking about."

"Well . . . what did you want to say in your song?"

Noah thought a moment. "I wanted to say . . . that I was sad when Justus died, but I know it was for the best because he was in pain and he couldn't get around anymore. And I miss him a lot, but I think—or at least *hope*—I'll see him in heaven." He lowered his voice. "I'm not sure about that. Do you think dogs go to heaven?"

"Beats me." Paige shrugged. "But I know there are animals there because Jesus comes back to earth on a white horse. And the new heaven and the new earth will have creations even better than this one. And Jesus

Liane

wants heaven to be perfect for us . . . so yeah, why can't dogs be there?"

"But . . . do you think Justus will be there?"

Paige's voice softened. "No clue, Noah. God loves us, and because he's promised that heaven will be an awesome place, maybe Justus will be there. But I do know this—you can trust God. You don't have to worry one minute about heaven."

Noah cleared his throat. His eyes had begun to water again. If they kept talking about Jussy, he'd soon be crying.

A smile suddenly lit up Paige's face. "So—you told me one of the things you want to say is that you were sad. But you can't write a line that says 'I was sad,' because that's *telling* the listener how you felt. You have to *show* the listener how you felt through a word picture."

Noah grunted. "Now you've really lost me."

She laughed. "Think a minute—what are some word pictures that show sadness?"

Noah leaned forward and scratched his chin. "You mean . . . like a kid chasing a kite that's flown away?"

She shook her head. "Not sad enough—he could think chasing the kite is fun. Can you think of something else?"

"Um . . . a football fan crying in the stadium when his team just lost the Super Bowl?"

"That's closer . . . but that's still not sad to everyone. Too many people couldn't care less who wins the Super Bowl."

"Okay. How about . . ." He shuddered as a memory rose in his mind. "How about a kid who comes downstairs to find a note saying his dad is moving away?"

Paige pressed her lips together. "That's better. Everyone would think *that's* sad. Most people can relate to losing someone."

"Okay." Noah straightened and pulled the notebook closer to his chest. "Thanks, Paige. You've given me a good place to start."

They looked up as the hotel doors slid open again. Liane walked out, wearing a grumpy look as she squinted into the morning sun. The others would be trickling out soon, then they'd be on the road again, bound to whatever gig filled this square on their monthly calendar.

Noah stood, then grabbed Paige's hand to guide her up. She had given him a big head start this morning—the least he could do was walk her to the bus.

17

As she boarded the bus, Liane spied a bulging bag of fan mail on the front seat. RC must have picked it up at the hotel desk last night so they'd have it on the bus this morning.

Sighing, she moved to the bag, opened the drawstring, and pulled out a handful of letters. Most of them had been addressed to YB2 in general or Shane Clawson in particular, but a few of the letters were addressed to Noah, Josiah, and Paige.

After the release of that *People* article, she didn't expect ever again to find a letter with her name on it. Still, some of these letters could have been written weeks ago, because they stacked up in the fan mail post office box until someone from Melisma Records forwarded them to the group while they were on the road.

There was no way they could personally answer every

letter. But because RC believed it was important to acknowledge the fans' support, he made sure each letter was answered—usually a glossy postcard featuring a black-and-white group publicity shot. In order to maintain a personal touch, however, he required each member of YB2 to answer seven letters per week. The responses didn't have to be long or complicated, just handwritten and autographed.

Sorting through the bag, Liane selected four letters addressed to YB2, and actually found three addressed to her—probably from kids who didn't read *People* or visit the YB2 chat room. After dropping them in her tote bag, she climbed into the second seat and curled up to wait for the others.

She lifted her head when Taz climbed aboard. As their resident techno expert, she knew he spent a lot of time in chat rooms with other computer whizzes.

"Hey, Taz." She pulled her notebook from her tote bag and flipped it to the first page. She pointed to the word she had copied from her computer screen: *hlolarawchawmp*. "Can you tell me what this means?"

Taz paused in the aisle and squinted at the word on the page. "Did you read this in a book somewhere?"

She glanced around, then lowered her voice. "I saw it in the YB2 chat room."

He laughed. "Oh—now it makes sense. That means 'hysterically laughing out loud and rolling around while clapping hands and wetting my pants.'"

Liane groaned. "So . . . this person was laughing."

"Howling, I'd say."

"Hmm." She shook her head and closed her notebook. "Thanks for the info."

Within an hour, Larry sat behind the wheel as the bus zoomed over the highway. RC wanted to get to their next gig early to practice the Spanish version of "Y B Alone?". Aunt Rhonda had faxed a pronunciation guide and the translated lyrics last night; Liane had a copy of the pages in her bag. She knew she ought to be studying her latest assignment, but she couldn't seem to get in the mood.

In the front seat, Paige was answering fan mail, too, dictating her responses to RC, who wrote her words on pretty, personalized stationery. Shane sat in the seat across from Paige, a copy of the Spanish lyrics in his hand. He and the others had it easy—all they had to do was echo a few words on the chorus. Liane had to carry the burden of the performance. Why? Because she was *smart*.

Her stomach twisted. She used to enjoy being one of the smartest kids in her class, but everything had changed when she joined YB2. At home she was Liane Nelson, daughter of Tom and Sharon, science fair finalist, honor student, and choir member. Here she was Liane of YB2, the lucky girl who sang between Shane and Noah. She knew the drill backward, forward, and inside out and could almost hear RC and Rhonda: "Liane and Paige are role models to thousands of girls who look to YB2 for guidance on their clothes, their attitudes, and their looks." The average American teenager couldn't relate

Liane

to an Einstein, so she had to be approachable, down-to-earth . . . well, normal. She owed it to their fans.

With these thoughts swirling in her brain, Liane pulled the fan letters out of her bag, then dug for her stationery.

To the four fans who'd written YB2, she thanked them for writing, said she hoped to see them at a concert near their city, and told them to never stop believing in God.

The first two letters to her were typical ("Oh, I love you! I love your music!"), and they'd been written by preteen girls who dreamed of singing with YB2. Liane sent them each a polite response, then signed her name with a flourish.

She was ready to write a basic reply to the last letter, but its words made her pause:

> *Dear Liane,*
>
> *I read about u in* People *magazine, and I knew there was a reason I liked u! I love smart people! I love your music, I like the way u sing, and u are my favorite. Where are u from? Do u have brothers and sisters? Do u want to go to college? Do u want to be a doctor?*
>
> *I am ten years old and I wish I could be just like u. Keep singing because I am your hugest fan. My biggest wish is that we will meet someday soon.*
>
> *Write back if u can.*
>
> *Bethany Baker*

Liane stared at the neatly typed page in disbelief. This girl had read Huck Phillips's diva comments and still *liked* her? She hadn't been turned off? Liane shook her head. Wow.

She chewed on the end of her pen as she considered what to say, then began to write:

Dear Bethany,

Thank you so much for writing. I like you too, and I will try to answer your questions.

I am from a small town outside Minneapolis, Minnesota. I will go to college someday, but I'm not sure what I will study. Sometimes I am interested in medicine, sometimes astronomy, but I am interested in all sorts of things.

Right now I am mainly interested in singing with YB2 and being an ordinary girl. You are ten and I am fourteen—why don't we enjoy being our age and worry about college later? :)

I am not sure if we will be able to meet—I am very busy with YB2, and we travel all over the place. Sometimes I don't even know where we are when we get off the bus! But if we come to your town, I hope you will come to the concert.

Thank you again for writing. Never stop believing! And one more thing—don't believe everything you read in print.

Your friend,
Liane Nelson

After signing the letter, Liane put it in an envelope, copied Bethany's address onto the front, and sealed it. She gathered it with the others, then walked to the front of the bus and dropped her letters into the bag for outgoing mail. The bag would be returned to Melisma Records, where someone would sort the letters and mail them.

With her letter-writing obligation fulfilled, Liane went back to her seat and picked up the novel she'd been trying to finish. The book was about a rich girl named Jordan who was having trouble fitting in with the other girls at her new school. Even though she didn't come from a rich family like the main character, Liane was beginning to think she and Jordan had a lot in common.

18

After retreating to the back of the bus, Noah pulled out his paper and pencil and gazed at the blank page. "Blank" seemed to describe *him* these days—he couldn't come up with anything for the song he wanted to write, he couldn't stop feeling sad about the loss of Jussy, and lately he'd been thinking a lot about his dad.

Jussy's death had probably brought on the dad thoughts. The dog had been a gift from Dad, so it was only natural that the dog's death would make Noah think about the man who had walked out of his life a few days after the puppy's arrival.

Noah stretched out on the carpeted floor and leaned against the bathroom door.

What was his dad doing in Las Vegas? What sort of job did he have? Had he met another woman, started another family? He'd been a car salesman in California, so was he

Liane

selling cars in Las Vegas, or had he moved on to something else?

Maybe he was selling computers . . . or dealing cards at one of the casinos. Mom would have a fit if she knew Noah even thought about all that, but a guy had to wonder. If Dad hadn't been drawn to the casinos, why would he have wanted to run to Las Vegas?

Maybe the other woman lived there, if she existed. If Dad had met someone new and she had kids, did Dad take them to ball games and amusement parks? Did he watch TV with them in the evening or go to their school concerts? He hadn't done any of those things with Noah. He'd always been too busy working to spend time at home, even at night after dinner.

He lowered his head as the old sadness crept over him like a fog. Noah's mom was constantly saying that the divorce wasn't Noah's fault; he hadn't done anything to make his dad leave. Still, if Noah'd been a jock instead of a musician, maybe his dad would've been prouder . . . and maybe he would've stayed. If Mom had wanted more kids, maybe his dad would've felt more obligated to stick it out.

But she hadn't, and he hadn't, and Noah still didn't understand exactly what had gone wrong. One week Dad came home with a puppy and Noah had been convinced his father was the best dad in the entire universe. The next week Dad packed a suitcase and left town, leaving Mom with the name of a lawyer, an envelope filled with a few hundred-dollar bills, and a confused son.

Noah clenched his fist as tears stung his eyes again. Good grief, he'd been crying more in the last few days than he had in years. What was the deal?

"God," he whispered, knocking his fist against his forehead, "you've gotta help me get a hold of myself. I can't stop thinking these thoughts, and they're driving me crazy. I can't be a good team member, I can't write this dumb song, and I can't seem to get a grip."

He waited, but there was no answering whisper, no boom of thunder, no crack of lightning outside the bus. There was only the growl of the engine and the occasional shifting of the gears as the bus rolled over the highway.

And then . . . Noah heard it. Not with his ears, exactly, but with his heart. A sure, strong voice that seemed to come from someplace outside himself.

Rest in me.

And in that moment, Noah knew he'd been searching for answers in all the wrong places. He'd been trying to find strength and wisdom in himself, yet what had RC said? Wisdom didn't come from books or formulas or structure or rhyme . . . wisdom came from God. And being God-smart is always better than being human-smart.

Noah hadn't lost his father. His earthly dad may have stepped out of the picture, but Noah still had a heavenly father who looked after him 24/7. He also had RC, who almost always had time to talk, and he had new friends who were closer than any brothers or sisters he might have had at home.

Maybe he needed to think about what God would want to say through his song.

That was the best idea he'd had in days.

Picking up his pencil, he hummed a measure of melody, then licked the tip of the lead and scrawled his title across the blank page. He'd been thinking about title ideas all morning, and this one seemed better than any of the others.

Now—how could he write a chorus that actually meant something?

He remembered what Paige had said about showing, not telling, so he jotted several word picture ideas in the margins of his page. All of them had possibilities, but he could only use two or three of the best ones. If he used too many, he'd be writing an opera, not a song.

An hour later, he heard the steady *thump-thump* of Paige's hand as she counted the backs of the bus seats. She was coming his way, probably headed to the bathroom, which meant he'd have to move out of her way.

"There you are." She paused in front of him. "How's the song coming?"

He smiled up at her. "Don't tell me you can still smell my cologne."

"Sometimes I can, yeah, but not right now. I figured you'd be back here where it's quiet."

"Well . . . I think it's coming. I've got a title, and I'm trying to figure out what—you know, what will illustrate it."

"Do you want to tell me the title?"

He shook his head. "Let me think on it a few days. When it's all ready, I'll let you know."

She grinned. "I know what you mean. I don't like to let anyone see my songs while they're under construction. I have to let Shane see them if he's helping me, but sometimes I like to keep things to myself, if you know what I mean."

"I think I know."

"Well, you know where to find me if you need help."

Holding on to the edge of the bunk, she turned around and walked back to the front of the bus.

Noah smiled as he recognized the tune she was softly singing: "Lean on Me."

19

Aunt Rhonda rarely scheduled concerts on
Sundays, so when the second Sunday of September rolled
around, Liane was grateful the group was safely tucked
away in a Hilton hotel outside Birmingham, Alabama.
The night before, they had performed in front of sixteen
thousand fans at the Birmingham-Jefferson Civic Center.
The concert had been lots of fun, the interviews with
local radio stations had gone well, and at the quick meet-
and-greet before the show, Liane had been pleased to see
that Josiah had become a fan favorite.

No one had been clamoring to meet her, of course. A
couple of girls from a school for the blind had won tickets
to meet Paige, but there were no local Einsteins or divas
who wanted to meet a fellow astronomer/snob-in-train-
ing. Paige had signed her name to a dozen black-and-
white glossies that appeared on a table, then she'd tossed

the Sharpie to Noah and said she'd meet the others in the greenroom.

With the morning off, she and Paige had slept late and ordered breakfast in their room. Now they pulled their Bibles from their suitcases and went down the hall to RC's suite, where they'd join the others for a worship service.

Liane knocked on the door, then grinned when Josiah let her in. "'Bout time," he said, moving aside so they could enter. Liane let Paige walk through first, then stopped next to Josiah. She made a face when she looked around the room and realized she and Paige were the last to arrive.

"Are we late?" she asked, hurrying forward. She sank into the sofa beside Taz. The twenty-year-old sound engineer had selected a blue do-rag for the occasion.

"Nah, you're cool," Noah answered, propping his feet on the ottoman. "Me 'n Shane got here early, and Taz and Josiah came right after."

Liane lifted her head as RC came out of the bedroom. Because it would be an official day off, he wore a cotton sweater and casual jeans.

"Good morning, girls." He tossed a quick smile in Liane's direction, then reached out to squeeze Paige's hand. "Everything okay?"

"Everything's great," Paige answered, dropping onto the sofa cushions between Noah and Shane. "Fine as frog hair."

Taz elbowed Liane. "Where *does* she get those sayings?"

"I think it's Southern," Liane answered in a stage whisper. "And we *are* in Alabama."

RC moved a desk chair into the circle, then turned it backward and straddled it. "Okay," he said, resting his arms on the back of the chair. "Time for worship." He nodded at Shane. "You want to lead us in a chorus?"

If Shane minded, Liane couldn't tell. He tapped his leg and began to sing a praise song; one by one, the others joined in.

While she sang, Liane closed her eyes and tried to lift her thoughts above the hotel room, the day, and all the problems that had been getting her down. Life could be so complicated—surely it didn't have to be that way! She had it good and knew she ought to be grateful. Out of thousands of girls who could have filled this spot in YB2, God had allowed her to be chosen—he had put her in this group for a reason.

He had even allowed Huck Phillips to interview her and print that awful story.

Liane's eyes flew open at the sudden realization. *Why would God allow such a horrible thing?*

She didn't have time to wonder. When the chorus ended, RC nodded toward Taz.

"I've asked Taz to lead us in a devotion today. Taz? Take it away."

The pages of Taz's thin black Bible rustled as he turned them. "I wasn't sure what I was supposed to say, but last night I read this psalm and thought you all might like to hear it." He cleared his throat, then began to read from Psalm 139:

"O Lord, you have examined my heart
and know everything about me.
You know when I sit down or stand up.
You know my every thought when far away.
You chart the path ahead of me
and tell me where to stop and rest.
Every moment you know where I am.
You know what I am going to say
even before I say it, Lord. . . .
To you the night shines as bright as day.
Darkness and light are both alike to you."

"Okay." Taz lowered his Bible and looked around the circle. "What does that passage mean to you?"

Silence followed, then Paige lifted her head. "I like that psalm," she said, "because I'm always in the dark, and I like knowing that darkness and light are the same to God. He can see what I can't, and he keeps me safe."

"I think," Josiah added, "it also means that God knows us better than anyone else ever could. He knows what I do now *and* what I'm going to do next week."

Noah slapped his chest. "Man! That's kinda scary."

Taz nodded. "Yeah, it is. God knows even the ugly parts of us, yet he loves us and he'll never leave us. No matter where we go in the bus or on a jet, God is always with us. He's with us in the recording studio, on the concert stage, in the rehearsal hall. And when we think no one else sees . . . he's still there. And he looks at our hearts, so he sees things about us nobody else can."

Liane

Taz closed his Bible. "A lot of people back in my neighborhood couldn't believe it when I said I was going to travel the country with a bunch of white folks. They didn't think I'd be respected in a white band." His gaze fell to the floor as a slow smile lit his face. "But you know what? They weren't thinkin' about all we have in common . . . they were only thinkin' about our differences. I'm black, you're white, but that's not nearly as important as the fact that we're all brothers and sisters under the skin. 'Cause Jesus makes us family."

His brown eyes went around the circle, resting for a moment on each team member. "I've come to love each of you guys just like my own family, but I still don't know everything about you. He looks behind our masks, ya know?"

Liane felt the pressure of someone's gaze and looked up to see Noah looking at her. He widened his eyes slightly as if trying to send her a message, but she glanced away.

At the moment, she wasn't interested in anything he had to say.

"You have nothing to fear by letting your real self shine," Taz continued. "Jesus loves you for who you are. And the people who matter will love you, too. If they don't—well, not everyone in the world loved Jesus, either. And I'm cool with that as long as I'm cool with him."

Liane looked up to see RC watching her. Had she done something wrong *again?* She was beginning to feel like a field mouse with an eagle flying overhead. If she made one wrong move, someone in the group was going to pounce on her.

"Okay." Taz rubbed his hands together. "Does anyone have any special prayer requests?"

Josiah asked for prayer for his family; Shane asked for prayer because he'd been struggling with his algebra lessons and had to take an online test next week. Liane thought about asking everyone to pray for her as she learned the Spanish lyrics for the Latin Grammy Awards, but what was the use? They believed she could do it without any help at all.

Taz led them in prayer, asking the Lord for a safe and good week, then he lifted his head. "I want to leave you with one last thought," he said, "from Proverbs 21:2. It's this: 'People may think they are doing what is right, but the Lord examines the heart.'"

Liane lowered her eyes as she stood and helped Paige up from the couch. For some unknown reason, those words struck like a dart at her heart . . . but why? She wasn't doing anything wrong.

Not a single thing.

20

"Hey."

Liane looked up as Noah stepped in front of her, blocking her way through the hall with an outstretched hotel towel. Clearly, he'd been swimming—his shoulders were still speckled with water drops, and his swim trunks were dripping.

She sighed in exasperation. The boys had spent their free afternoon at the pool—she'd spent hers in the room memorizing a set of Spanish lyrics. "Hey, what?"

He draped the towel around his neck and stepped closer, glancing around. "What'd you think of Taz's devotion today?"

"You're dripping all over the carpet, Noah. You should use that towel for drying off."

"Nag, nag, nag. And you didn't answer my question."

Young Believer on Tour 127

Liane

She shrugged. "What was I supposed to think about it? I've heard that psalm a hundred times."

"Yeah . . . but what did it say to you?"

Frowning, she resisted the impulse to grab his towel and pop him with it. "What was it *supposed* to say?"

"Masks," Noah insisted. "He talked about wearing masks. And you've been wearing one ever since that stupid *People* article came out."

"I have not."

"Have too."

"Have not."

"Yes, you have."

She glared at him a minute, then shrugged. "So maybe I have. What's wrong with that? I'm not hurting anybody. I'm trying to be a role model and all that other stuff RC wants us to be. RC *wants* us to wear masks, or he wouldn't tell us to mind our manners when other people are around."

"How can you say you're not hurting anybody? You're suffocating yourself."

She snorted, then lowered her head and ducked under his outstretched arm, pushing him out of her way.

"Hey! No need to get violent about it." He fell into step beside her as she strode down the hall.

"No need to bring it up, was there?"

"I was only trying to help!"

"I don't need your help. I don't need anybody's help. I'm the genius girl, remember?"

He turned and blocked her way again, saying nothing,

as her words hung in the silence. Her anger faded when she saw hurt in his eyes—he really had been trying to do what was best for her. And she . . . well, she'd been as snappy with him as she'd been with everyone else lately.

"You're right, Noah," she finally said, her voice rough. "But I don't know how to fix my problem. People our age don't look up to smart kids. You know how it is—"

"Actually—" Noah scuffed the carpet with his bare foot—"I don't. The other guys always called me 'dumbhead' 'cause I had to get LD help." He barked a short laugh. "No one's ever accused me of being a whiz kid."

She softened her voice. "You're all right, Noah."

"So are you." He looked at her a minute longer, then smiled and slipped his arm around her shoulders. "You're not a diva, and you're not a snob. So come on, I'll walk you to your room."

She pushed at his rib cage, but gently. "Get away from me. You're wet."

"Only a little."

"A lot. Now scram."

She said nothing as he grinned and strolled away, but she would have given her last dollar to know what he was thinking.

21

That night, Liane lay in her bed in the hotel room and listened as the air conditioner turned on and off. She'd been lying there for an hour as Paige slept in the next bed. She ought to be sleeping herself, but she'd been in a mental wrestling match ever since she turned the light out and dropped her head to the pillow.

As the hour for the awards show drew nearer, Liane felt a new excitement flow through the team. The adrenaline always kicked in when they got up to sing before a packed audience, but the Latin Grammy Awards would be something special—first of all, it would be live on national television, and second, they were performing something completely different.

She'd already spent several hours listening to a native speaker repeat her Spanish words on tape, and she was up for the challenge even though she still resented RC's opinion that she was the only one bright enough to learn the lyrics. His decision would only focus more attention on her brains, and that wasn't fair. Sure, she would probably have less trouble learning the lyrics than Shane, Paige, Noah, or Josiah, but she didn't like being singled out. She'd be under a lot of pressure—not that she couldn't handle it—and the others hadn't been asked to handle the same kind of stress. That wasn't right . . . was it?

On Tuesday night, huge portions of the world would be watching the show . . . including all the people who'd read Huck Phillips's article and were convinced she was a walking, talking diva with an overblown cerebellum. If she sang the Spanish lyrics without a single mistake, they'd shake their heads and say, "Yep. The girl's an Einstein, all right. No wonder she's a snob." But if she happened to forget a line or two . . . or even an entire verse . . .

The world wouldn't think she was so smart then, would they? The millions of Americans who didn't speak Spanish wouldn't know she'd messed things up—unless she stopped singing and rolled her eyes to the ceiling or something. If she stopped singing and made faces, the other singers would freak because they were depending on her to feed them the words. Suddenly they'd have to come up with the words on their own, and they'd understand how it felt to have the pressure of an entire performance dumped on your shoulders.

If she bombed, no one outside the group would be too

terribly upset. Most people would just say, "Hey, she's only a fourteen-year-old girl. You can't expect an ordinary kid to sing a foreign language perfectly on live television."

And that's what they'd think she was—an ordinary girl who had been totally misrepresented by a magazine reporter.

And a mistake, even a major one, wouldn't hurt her career or anything. RC would be upset for a while, but he'd get over it. He'd have to forgive her, and he might even feel bad about asking so much of her.

Making a royal mess of things would only hurt her reputation as a diva genius . . . and that was the entire point, wasn't it?

Looking into the darkness, she considered her options. This afternoon in rehearsal, she'd sung the Spanish words perfectly, but she'd been holding the printed lyrics in her hand. She wouldn't be holding the words in the real performance. She wouldn't even have them printed on a teleprompter, so it'd look completely natural if she stared out at the lights and . . . went blank. Forgetfulness happened to everybody at one time or another. Even professionals like Barbra Streisand were sometimes afflicted with stage fright.

So who could blame her if she developed a sudden case of blank brain on live television?

22

Tuesday, September 14

"Why is being fourteen so hard? Why can't I decide what to do?" Liane studied her reflection in the mirror, but the wide-eyed girl in the glass didn't answer. Frustrated, Liane threw her hairbrush in the sink and backed away.

She was alone in one of the locker rooms at the AmericanAirlines Arena in Miami, dressed for the performance in her black shirt, and *still* uncertain of how she should perform at the Latin Grammys. She had changed her mind again and again in the past two days. Now she had less than two hours before YB2's live performance, and she still didn't know what she should do. She knew the Spanish words to "Y B Alone?"; she could have recited them backward in her sleep. She *could* strut out on that stage, give the nation a picture-perfect performance, and make everybody happy.

But delivering a flawless performance would prove everything Huck Phillips had written. And some smart aleck TV commentator or the emcee was likely to comment on what a quick study she was and how perfect her diction had been. And someone else would remark, "Well, I hear she's a bit of a diva. At fourteen—can you imagine?"

If she sang well, she'd be considered a stuck-up bulbous brain forever.

On the other hand, if she went onstage and sang "adios amigo" or some other nonsense over and over, her teammates would be flabbergasted, they might mess up, and RC would be *furious*—at least for a while. He believed in excellence, and he expected 110 percent at every performance. Still . . . he hadn't been very understanding about her problem with the *People* article.

Every time she closed her eyes, she could see his face, his eyes begging her to listen as he explained the difference between God-smart and human-smart. . . .

There it was again. The tug on her heart, telling her to do the right thing.

But why did Christians always have to do the right thing? She'd been doing the right thing most of her life. She'd never been in any serious trouble, never been a bad kid. When her friends back home had cheated on tests, she had studied harder, determined to make good grades without cheating. When one of her other girlfriends had stolen a pair of earrings at the mall, Liane had told her parents all about what happened, then quietly pulled away from that friendship.

She'd been a good girl forever . . . wasn't she allowed to do *something* for herself? After all, Jesus would forgive her . . . and so would RC. And her parents might not ever realize that she'd goofed up on purpose.

If she blew her lines, people would think she was a normal teenager who made a mistake. They might think she was lazy, but the people who really knew her would know better. They'd chalk her mistake up to too much pressure.

If she pretended to go blank, people would excuse her. Whenever kids in the Olympics made mistakes, sports announcers were quick to offer excuses and divert the attention elsewhere.

What should she do?

She was about to run through her list of pros and cons again when someone knocked on the outer door.

"Lee, you in there?"

She recognized Shane's voice. "Yeah—you need something?"

"You decent?"

"Of course."

He opened the door and peeked around the corner at her. "You'd better come on out. RC's waiting for us in the greenroom. Those people from the Make-A-Wish Foundation will be here any minute."

Liane bit back a groan. She didn't mind meeting the kids, but right now she had more important things to think about.

But RC would be waiting, and she couldn't make *two* major mistakes in a single day.

She waved at Shane over her shoulder. "I'll be there in a minute."

She gave her face a quick once-over in the mirror, then stuffed her brush and makeup into her tote bag and followed Shane. The greenroom was next to the girls' dressing room, and Paige, Noah, and Josiah were waiting inside with RC. Like Liane, they had already dressed in the black leather performance outfits they'd wear for the television show, because RC wanted YB2 to look their best for the kids from Make-A-Wish.

Last year they had met their first group of Make-A-Wish kids. Liane had heard of the program before she joined YB2, but she had never dreamed that a dying girl's greatest wish would be for an opportunity to meet her. But last year three young cancer patients had expressed a wish to meet YB2, and on three separate occasions the team had met the kids, eaten dinner with them, and called them onto the stage during concerts. Each time, the brave young patients had received a standing ovation from the crowd.

Tonight's situation was a little different—YB2 wouldn't be able to call these children to the stage during the Latin Grammys, but RC said they should still feel honored that three children in the Miami area had wished for a meeting with YB2.

Liane had just slipped into an empty chair next to Paige when the door swung open. A security guard stepped forward to check the visitors' ID badges, then three sets of parents entered, each with a child between them.

Liane couldn't be sure, but she guessed the first two children, a boy and a girl, were cancer patients. Each of them wore scarves around their heads. She thought they had probably lost their hair from chemotherapy. They both had the slightly puffy look she recognized as a side effect of drugs that kept their bodies from rejecting donated bone marrow or an organ.

The sight of the third child, a girl, caught Liane off guard. The girl stood no more than three feet tall and had arms and legs as thin as matchsticks. She wore a covering on her head, too, but she wasn't completely bald. Liane could see thin wisps of white hair beneath the brim of the tiny straw hat the girl wore.

Her big eyes were a faded blue, her features sharp and bony. But a smile lit her face, and when she looked into the room her eyes locked with Liane's as though she didn't care one bit about any of the others.

"Liane!" she crowed in a crackling voice that reminded Liane of her grandma. Then she slipped free of her parents and ran to Liane, who stood just in time to feel the girl's thin arms lock around her waist.

Not knowing what else to do, Liane returned the girl's hug, then cast a questioning look at the parents.

The mother stepped forward, an apologetic smile on her face. "This is Bethany," she said, "and we can't believe the timing of all this. For months she's been praying that she'd get this chance to meet you, and then yesterday she got your letter. So she gets a visit and a personally signed letter all at once—I tell you, this has been the best week of her life!"

Her letter? What in the world was this woman talking about?

Speechless, Liane looked down as the little girl pulled away and looked up, her eyes shining. "I'm Bethany Baker," she said in her birdlike voice. "I wrote you, remember? And you wrote me back."

Liane nodded, trying to place the name. She couldn't remember writing this girl, and she couldn't figure out what had happened to make her look so old and frail. This girl didn't look like the other cancer patients they had met, nor did she look like someone with muscular dystrophy or cerebral palsy . . .

"I said I was your hugest fan, and you said you weren't sure if we'd ever get to meet. But I told the people at the foundation that meeting you was my biggest wish, and now it has come true!"

Liane struggled for words. "Why . . . that's wonderful!"

As the other two kids gravitated to the table where Shane, Josiah, Noah, and Paige were autographing pictures for them, Bethany took Liane's hands and pulled her onto the couch against the wall. "I think you're the absolute *best*," she said, accenting the word with a broad smile.

Liane forced a laugh. "That's very sweet, Bethany. I'm glad somebody thinks so."

The girl's mouth dropped open. "Come on . . . everybody does!"

"Not everybody." Liane smiled at the parents, who were beaming at their strange little girl. "Lots of people think I'm some sort of geek with a diva attitude. Haven't you seen the latest headlines in *Tiger Beat*?"

Bethany's thin mouth clamped tight for a moment, then her head bobbed forward in a nod. "Oh, that. Nobody believes all that stuff, Liane. Why—we need smart people like you! My doctors are always saying we need more scientists and researchers to help kids like me. They're close to finding a cure and treatment for my disease, but they're not close enough. And that's why I like you—because someday you might go into research and find something that will help kids."

Liane stared at the girl. "What disease?" she whispered. Feeling awkward and embarrassed, she looked toward the girl's father. "What's wrong with her?"

"Bethany suffers from progeria," the father said. His eyes crinkled at the corners as he explained. "It's fairly rare; at any given time there are probably fewer than 100 affected children in the world."

"What . . . what does it do?"

"It's premature aging." Bethany's mother sank onto the sofa next to her daughter. "Kids who have it grow old seven times faster than other children their age. They don't grow *up*—height-wise—they just grow old."

Bethany squeezed Liane's hands. "I'm ten years old, Liane. But my muscles and bones feel like they're seventy."

Liane felt her heart do a double beat. If this girl's body was seventy in biological years . . . Bethany Baker was rapidly nearing the end of her life. So when she said she wanted Liane to help others, she meant it. She wouldn't live long enough for Liane to grow up and learn enough to help her.

The realization left Liane speechless.

Spurred by an impulse from someplace deep inside her, Liane reached over and gently drew Bethany into her arms. The tiny girl relaxed as a happy sigh escaped her lips, and in that moment Liane knew what she had to do on the stage tonight . . . and what she'd been doing wrong.

"Okay, gang, can I have your attention?" RC clapped his hands and grinned, his enthusiasm shining in his eyes. "This should be a fun gig. We're scheduled to take the stage at 9:10 P.M., if all goes according to the master plan." His smile tightened a little. "These people run an organized program. I have the feeling we'll be on exactly as scheduled. The director doesn't seem to like surprises."

RC didn't like surprises, either.

Liane looked down at Bethany, who sat beside her on the couch, her little hand tucked into the crook of Liane's elbow. The girl's simple faith touched a deep place in Liane's heart—a place not even critics or magazine reporters could reach.

Bethany Baker believed Liane could make a difference in the world of medicine . . . and not everyone could do that. Only someone with determination and intelligence and stubborn curiosity would even think about trying to cure a life-threatening disease that affected fewer than 100 children at any given moment.

Like it or not, Liane knew she was one of those kinds of people. She could turn her curiosity from black holes to progeria, from quarks to chromosomes. Someday, when she had finished college and earned a medical degree, she could figure out what caused progeria, and then work to cure it. And then there would be *no* children affected with this terrible illness . . . and Bethany Baker's truest and greatest wish would come true.

Liane closed her eyes, only half-listening to RC as he rambled on about the beginnings of YB2 for the sake of the visiting children and their parents.

How stupid she'd been! For the last few days she'd been pretending to be something she wasn't, thinking that she would give a bad performance for the sake of the group's image, when it was actually her own pride that was most important to her. She'd told herself she needed to be ordinary so other kids could relate to her, but when she'd tried to be "ordinary," she'd only acted giddy and foolish.

She didn't need to act as thick as a plank to win other people's approval . . . and why was she trying to please other teenagers, anyway? God had created her with a curious mind and a great memory for a reason, and he'd placed her in YB2. Being fake with their fans would mean denying the way God made her. And that wasn't right.

God had put her in this place at the perfect time. He had led her to Bethany. He had even arranged the interview with Huck Phillips . . . and now she understood why.

But one thing still confused her. She had answered

Bethany's letter only four days ago. Her response had gone into the big mailbag, and those letters would have gone to Melisma Records, where the mail clerks usually took a week to sort through them and mail the replies. So how did Bethany get hers so quickly?

She looked around the group, trying to think of an explanation. Perhaps the letter had fallen out of the mailbag. Perhaps someone else—maybe RC?—had picked it up and dropped it in a regular mailbox. Who knew?

But the odds of that happening were slim, and Liane was sure she'd dropped Bethany's letter into the mailbag with the others. God sure worked in mysterious ways . . .

She felt a gentle squeeze on her elbow and looked down to see Bethany looking at her, trust and adoration shining in those big blue eyes.

"Thank you for coming, Bethany," Liane whispered, giving the girl's hand a return squeeze. "I will absolutely never forget you."

23

"And now," *the announcer said,* his voice booming through the speakers, "without further ado, let me present America's hottest singing sensations and our honored guests—YB2!"

As the music began, Liane strutted onto the stage, her heart pounding to the rhythm. Taz had added a Latin beat to the background track for "Y B Alone?" and the sound added an entirely new spin to the song. The other singers moved to the back line as Liane stepped forward, ready to carry the song on live national television.

It would be so easy to mess it up.

So easy to "forget" and sing in English.

So easy to wear a mask and be false to her true self.

But God didn't want her to wear a mask—and her future would unfold according to his master plan.

Liane

Stepping out in confidence, she opened her mouth and began to sing:

"Tú dices que tienes el corazón en pedazos,
Tú dices que estás sola,
¿Por qué te quedas en la oscuridad
Cuando hay amor en Su corazón
Para tocarte . . . y para abrazarte?
Tú dices que tu vida es una pérdida de tiempo,
Tú dices que apenas puedes vivir.
¿Por qué escuchas esas mentiras
Cuando hay amor en Sus ojos
Para atraerte . . . y guardarte?"

Gathering her courage, she increased the volume on the chorus: "Porque sé," she sang, as the others echoed.
". . . (sí, lo sé),
Quien es la fuente de amor
Y lo sé (sí, lo sé)
Quien nos brinda el poder.
No lo es (no, no es)
La estrella de TV
Es Dios . . .
Quien a todos creó."

As she stepped out to sing the second verse, she turned to smile at Paige, feeling the beat at the keys.

"Tú dices que todo te va bien ahora,
Tú dices que eres fuerte.
Asegúrate de que estás parada en tierra firme.

Liane

Sólo en la Roca te encuentras la esperanza,
Y esa esperanza es . . . para siempre."

She turned in a circle, feeling the joy of the song, and the audience surprised her by singing along on the chorus:

"Porque sé (sí, lo sé)
Quien es la fuente de amor
Y lo sé (sí, lo sé)
Quien nos brinda el poder.
No lo es (no, no es)
El rico y su dinero,
Es Dios . . .
Quien a todos creó."

Breathless, she sang the bridge to Noah:

"Es El quien desea amarte
(¿Por qué estás sola?)
Siempre está a tu lado
(Nunca estás sola)
Nunca dejes de creer
(El nunca te abandona)
El te llama por tu nombre
(Hoy y para siempre)."

"Porque sé," the world sang with her. When she turned back to the crowd, the entire audience was singing along.

". . . (sí, lo sé),
Quien es la fuente de amor

Y lo sé (sí, lo sé)
Quien nos brinda el poder.
No lo es (no, no es)
Los expertos del mundo,
Es Dios . . .
Quien a todos creó."

Grinning, Liane stepped to the back line, grabbed Paige's and Noah's hands, then threw herself into the bow, her heart pounding with delight.

24

Sighing in relief, Liane led the others offstage. When they had slipped behind the soundproof stage doors, they celebrated with whoops, hugs, and high fives.

"Way to go, Lee!" Paige thrust her hand into the air and waited for Liane to slap it. "Great job!"

"Come on, everyone," RC said, gesturing toward the door, "we need to clear this area for the other acts."

Liane breathed deeply as they walked back to the greenroom where snacks and soft drinks waited. Other celebrities had crowded into the room, and Liane giggled as Shane and Noah made a beeline for Nelly Furtado, who was waiting for her appearance.

Liane picked up a bottle of water, then walked back to the door to find the Baker family. Mr. and Mrs. Baker had promised to bring Bethany back to the greenroom after the show so the girls could say good-bye.

When the family came through the doorway, Liane gestured to a quiet corner in the hallway. "It's too noisy in there," she explained, leading the way out of the greenroom. Once the Bakers had followed, she knelt on one knee and looked into Bethany's eyes. How strange—this tiny girl was only four years younger than she was, but in some ways she seemed years older. Not in physical age . . . but in being God-smart.

In knowing what mattered.

"Bethany." Liane squeezed the girl's shoulder. "Thank you so much for making me your greatest wish. You've given me something very special by coming here today."

A look of doubt flashed across the girl's face. "Oh, I couldn't give you anything. You're . . . you're everything, Liane. You're pretty and smart and nice and talented—"

"Thank you, but—" Liane paused to search for words. "You may not understand this, but before you came here today, I was feeling bad about being different—you know, about being interested in things that don't interest other girls my age. But you've helped me see things better. And I think you're pretty cool . . . because you see the big picture, just like God does."

Bethany nodded, her eyes grave. "I know what you mean," she whispered. "I don't fit in with kids my age, either. They're all busy being silly and playing games and worrying about stupid stuff—I do that too, sometimes, but I also worry about living . . . and dying. I know I'm going to heaven when I die, but I worry about leaving my parents alone." She threw her arms around Liane's neck.

"I was praying you'd be as nice as you looked in your pictures. I'm so glad you are!"

Breathing a sigh of relief, Liane was glad, too—that she hadn't been foolish enough to break this girl's heart.

25

Tired but happy, the entire team piled back on the bus after changing into street clothes. As Noah carried the totes aboard the bus, he noticed that Liane seemed cheerful and more like her old self . . . a good thing.

"Hey, Noah." She grinned at him as he passed by her seat. "It was a fun gig, wasn't it?"

"Yeah." He nodded as he lifted the bags into the overhead luggage compartment. "Even though all we did was back you up."

Paige lifted her head. "Whatever we did, we sure sounded good doin' it."

"We looked good, too," Josiah added. "And I don't speak a word of Spanish. I think I could have fooled all the kids back home."

"Just don't try to speak it to anyone else," Shane warned. "They'll know you're an ignoramus."

Josiah made a face at Shane, then hurried away.

"I tried to say hi to Nelly Furtado," Noah said, wagging his brows at Liane. "I said, 'Hola, amigo,' and she laughed at me."

"You should have said *amiga*—you used the word you should say to a man."

"I don't get it." Noah shook his head. "In English, 'hello' works for everybody. Why do men and women have different hellos in Spanish?"

Liane winked at him. "'Hello' is the same. It's the 'friend' part that's different . . . and it's because men and women are different."

Noah sank into an empty seat, satisfied with this latest proof that Liane was back to normal. She was teaching everyone again, which meant she was no longer trying to act ditzy—

Which reminded him—

"Hey, everybody." He rose in his seat, then turned to face the others. "When we get on the road, I'd like to share something with you."

"Why wait?" Paige said, a knowing smile on her lips. "We'll be sitting here another twenty minutes, at least. Taz and the crew are still packing the equipment."

"Right." Noah held up a finger. "Okay, then. Everybody stay where you are and I'll be back in a minute."

He hurried through the bus to the bunk where he'd left his backpack, then pulled out his notebook. He'd stayed up late last night working on this project, but at last he thought he had a song worth sharing. This might not be a Grammy-winning tune, but it was a start.

He brought his notebook and guitar to the front of the bus, then turned and waited until the chatter died down.

Liane was the first to speak. "Go on, Noah. We're listening."

He cleared his throat as he glanced around at the others. "Lee's the one who gave me the idea to do this. Most of you know about what happened to Justus, and I've . . . well, I had a hard time dealing with it. So Liane said I should put all those feelings into something useful like a song. I couldn't get started, so Joe helped me with the poem."

He looked up at Josiah, who had gone the color of a cherry tomato.

Noah laughed. "Joe was a big help, but our poem wasn't quite right for lyrics, so Paige gave me some advice, too. Things finally started to come together when I realized that if I wanted to write a song to help others, well, not everybody has lost a dog. But lots of people have lost something or someone, and . . . well, I lost someone, too. So I wrote this song about Jussy . . . and about my dad."

He paused to swallow the lump that had risen in his throat. "This may not be the most beautiful song in the world, but God helped me do the best I could. So here it is."

He pulled his guitar from the floor, then settled it on

his knee. After propping his notebook against the back of the seat, he strummed a G chord and began to sing:

"I thought life would sorta flow by,
I never had much reason to cry,
Until you left me alone.
I thought I'd caught the golden ring,
Life offered me so many things,
Until my heart turned to stone."

He strummed double time for the chorus.

"Now now now, I'm trusting heaven alone,
Now I'm thinkin' 'bout another home,
Now I'm trading in my heart of stone,
I'm trusting heaven . . . heaven alone."

Accompanied by the low growl of the diesel engine, he sang the second verse:

"We always walked together down by the shore,
I gave you my heart, you're the one I adored,
Until you said 'so long.'
You were the only one I could always trust,
But when you left, oh something told me I must
Look toward something else. . . ."

Noah began to sing the chorus and smiled when Paige joined him in a light harmony:

"Now now now, I'm trusting heaven alone,
Now I'm thinkin' 'bout another home,
Now I'm trading in my heart of stone,
I'm trusting heaven . . . heaven alone."

Paige fell silent as he sang the bridge:

"Maybe you never meant to hurt me,
Maybe the future's dark and murky,
Maybe you never would desert me,
But I still miss you. . . ."

He moved into the chorus, and this time Paige,
Shane, and Josiah joined him.

"Now now now, I'm trusting heaven alone,
Now I'm thinkin' 'bout another home,
Now I'm trading in my heart of stone,
I'm trusting heaven . . . heaven alone."

He strummed the final chord, waited a moment,
then pressed his hand to the strings, stilling the sound.
A moment of silence filled the bus, then Liane began to
clap. As the others joined her, Noah sank into his seat,
his cheeks burning.

"That's wonderful," Paige said, leaning over the back
of the seat. "We could really do something with that."

"We could record it," Shane said. "Or maybe perform
it live, without tracks—just piano and acoustic guitar."

"It'd make a nice piece to open the second set," Liane added. "That song would establish a reflective mood."

"I think that's a good idea."

Recognizing RC's voice, Noah sank lower into his seat. The director must have entered the bus while he was singing and his back was to the door.

RC came forward and dropped his hand on Noah's shoulder. "I'm proud of you, Son. You faced a challenge and stuck with it. And you came up with a song that will speak to people."

Embarrassment mingled with pleasure as Noah looked toward Liane. "I hope so," he said, meeting her eyes. "I sure hope so."

26

Liane pulled her favorite old sweater from her tote bag and wadded it into a ball to serve as a pillow against the window. They had pulled out of the AmericanAirlines Arena and were back on the road, traveling up Interstate 95 toward Orlando—home to YB2.

She positioned the sweater beneath her cheek and stared out at the night sky, but this time her thoughts did not follow the stars. Instead she looked at the dim reflection in the glass and saw a girl who had momentarily lost her way.

"Never stop believin' . . ." She whispered the lyrics.

They sang those words in nearly every concert, but in the last few days she had stopped believing so many important things. For a supposedly smart girl, she'd done some pretty stupid things.

Taz was right—human-smart and God-smart were completely different.

But she'd learned something . . . and she would never stop believing that God had created her for a purpose. That purpose had nothing to do with pleasing others and everything to do with pleasing the One who had created her.

As the engines purred and drew her toward sleep, Liane closed her eyes and whispered a special prayer of thanks for Bethany Baker. That tiny girl's life—brief though it might be—shone with a brilliance and clarity far beyond anything Liane had ever known.

"Help her, God," Liane prayed. "And help me to always remember what she taught me tonight—wisdom often comes in small, unexpected packages."

Never Stop Believin'

Young man sittin' lost by a streetlight,
Countin' out his last thin dimes,
What was he thinkin' by comin' here,
What dreams shone in his dark eyes?
Young girl cryin' lost in a bare room,
Missin' folks she's left far behind,
Where is the life she longed for?
Young Cinderella must have been blind.

Chorus:
Hold on, he feels your broken heart's pain,
Stand strong, faith holds the key to rescue,
Reach out to love that cleanses your heart stains,
And never stop believin' . . . that God dreams of you.

Young man finds a book in a trash can,
Opens up to a promise so old,

Liane

Reads of love bigger than his heartbreak,
Reads of One who can heal his soul—
Cinderella hears a sound in the hallway,
Old woman standing at the door,
Hungry girl, let me warm and feed you,
I know just what you're lookin' for.

Chorus:
Hold on, he feels your broken heart's pain,
Stand strong, faith holds the key to rescue,
Reach out to love that cleanses your heart stains,
And never stop believin' . . . that God dreams of you.

Bridge:
I know you've dreamed of a true love,
(He's dreaming, too)
I know you've dreamed of a home,
(He's dreamed of you)
I know you've dreamed of forever,
(You know what to do).

Chorus:
Hold on, he feels your broken heart's pain,
Stand strong, faith holds the key to rescue,
Reach out to love that cleanses your heart stains,
And never stop believin' . . . that God dreams of you.

WORDS AND MUSIC BY SHANE CLAWSON
AND PAIGE CLAWSON, 2003.

Young Believer™ ON TOUR

Collect all 6 books in the Young Believer on Tour series!

1. **Josiah**

2. **Liane**

3. **Noah**

4. **Paige**

5. **Shane**

6. **Taz**

youngbeliever.com

TYNDALE KiDS

WheRe AdvEnture beGins with a BoOk!

LoG oN @ Cool2Read.com

NEVER STOP BELIEVING!

Have you ever wondered why Christians believe what they do? Or how you're supposed to figure out *what* to believe? Maybe you hear words and phrases and it seems like you're supposed to know what they mean. If you've ever thought about this stuff, then the *Young Believer Bible* is for you! There isn't another Bible like it.

The *Young Believer Bible* will help you understand what the Bible is about, what Christians believe, and how to act on what you've figured out. With dozens of "Can You Believe It?" and "That's a Fact!" notes that tell of the many crazy, miraculous, and hard-to-believe events in the Bible, hundreds of "Say What??" definitions of Christian words you'll hear people talk about, plus many more cool features, you will learn why it's important to . . . **Never stop believing!**

Ready for more?

Other items available in the Young Believer product line:

Young Believer Case Files

Be sure to check out
www.youngbeliever.com

How easy is it to live out your faith?

Sometimes it may seem as though no one is willing to stand up for God today. Well, *Young Believer Case Files* is here to prove that's simply not true!

Meet a group of young believers who had the guts to live out their Christian faith. Some of them had to make tough decisions, others had to hold on to God's promises during sickness or some other loss, and still others found courage to act on what God says is right, even when other people disagreed.

You can have the kind of powerful faith that makes a difference in your own life and in the lives of people around you.

The question is . . . how will YOU live out your faith?

Young Believer 365

Be sure to check out
www.youngbeliever.com

365?? You mean every day??
You'd better believe it!

Maybe you know something about the Bible . . . or maybe you don't. Maybe you know what Christians believe . . . or maybe it's new to you. It's impossible to know everything about the Bible and Christianity because God always has more to show us in his Word. *Young Believer 365* is a great way to learn more about who God is and what he's all about.

Through stories, Scripture verses, and ideas for how to live out your faith, this book will help you grow as a young believer. Experience God's power each day as you learn more about God's amazing love, his awesome plans, and his incredible promises for you.

Start today. See what God has in store for you!

Never stop believing!